The Unexpected Dream

by

NICOLE PYLAND

The Unexpected Dream

Sports Series Book #3

Mia Landis was so close to being an Olympian. Instead, she watched the Tokyo Olympics and her would-be-team from home with her one-year-old daughter. When Mia heard about a serious professional softball league starting up in the US, she thought it would be crazy to try out. After being convinced, though, she gave it a shot and ended up moving her entire life across the country.

Skylar Donahue lived for the game. Softball had been her entire world until an injury took away her shot to play in the Olympics. She resigned herself to coaching until she heard about a new league starting up. When she made the local team, she had no idea that a new woman in town would completely change her entire world.

Both women dreamed of representing their country in the Olympics. Neither of them thought their lives would take the turn they'd taken. But if they can see past what they thought their lives would be, and look at where they ended up, they might find a whole new dream; one that could last a lifetime.

To contact the author or for any additional information visit: **https://nicolepyland.com**

<u>BY THE AUTHOR</u>

Stand-alone books:

- The Fire
- The Moments
- The Disappeared
- Reality Check

Chicago Series:

- Introduction – Fresh Start
- Book #1 – The Best Lines
- Book #2 – Just Tell Her
- Book #3 – Love Walked into The Lantern
- Series Finale – What Happened After

San Francisco Series:

- Book #1 – Checking the Right Box
- Book #2 – Macon's Heart
- Book #3 – This Above All
- Series Finale – What Happened After

Tahoe Series:

- Book #1 – Keep Tahoe Blue

- Book #2 – Time of Day
- Book #3 – The Perfect View
- Book #4 – Begin Again
- Series Finale – What Happened After

Celebrities Series:

- Book #1 – No After You
- Book #2 – All the Love Songs

Sports Series:

- Book #1 – Always More
- Book #2 – A Shot at Gold
- Book #3 – The Unexpected Dream
- Book #4 – Finding a Keeper

CONTENTS

PROLOGUE

DURING the 1940s, the US and Japan made an attempt to get softball included in the Olympic Games. The efforts continued in the 1950s when the Amateur Softball Association of America sent letters to national organizations asking for assistance in getting the freshly minted International Olympic Federation to include softball in the upcoming games. These efforts continued into the 1960s as the International Softball Federation worked consistently towards the same goal. There was a requirement of the sport being played in at least eleven countries who could field teams to compete, and that the international governing body for the sport must have had at least twenty-nine national federations affiliated with it. Softball only had fifteen.

Efforts continued during the 1970s. The 1984 Olympics were held in the US, and the hope was that it would be at least considered as a demonstration or exhibition sport. When that didn't happen, the Barcelona Olympic Organizing Committee decided to make softball a demonstration sport at the 1992 Summer Olympics. The IOC said that because they felt its inclusion would be an "undue burden" on the organizers, it would not be included. Baseball, however, became a medal sport that year.

Finally, softball was introduced as an Olympic sport in the 1996 Summer Olympics in Atlanta, Georgia. Starting then, eight teams competed in the event every four years.

The US won three of the four gold medals and the silver in Beijing. They were a powerhouse team, bringing home trophies and medals in every tournament. It was sad, though, that the games in 2008 resulted in only a silver medal, because in 2005, the IOC voted to drop softball from the Olympic program for 2012 in London, and then again, in 2016 in Rio.

When players found out that their sport was being removed from the Olympics prior to Beijing, they were forced to develop fast to make their national teams by 2008, or else they'd lose out on their chance to live their dream and play *their* sport in the Olympic Games.

After eight years and two Summer Olympics, the IOC decided to put softball and its counterpart, baseball, back into the summer event. The Americans won the 2018 World Championship and, thus, were the very first team to qualify for the games. This was incredibly important to the players on the current roster, but also to those players who dreamed of making the national team of the future.

Mia Landis watched the gold medal match in Tokyo. Well, she wasn't *in* Tokyo. She was sitting in her living room with her one-year-old daughter sleeping against her chest. She had finally gotten Hazel to sleep after hours of trying, and, of course, just as the little girl had finally dozed off, the game was in the last inning. Mia wanted so badly to be there with her former teammates. She had grown up with many of them in the sport. She knew how much this moment would mean to them if they were able to bring home the nation's fourth gold medal in a sport most people had given up on. She looked down at her daughter with light-blonde baby hair and smiled. She was so happy she had this little one, but having her came with personal sacrifices. Mia had gotten pregnant and, despite being on the national team, had to give up her chance at these games to bring Hazel into the world. She had no regrets, of course, but she did have a wish. She wanted to be in Paris in 2024, competing for the United States of America.

THE UNEXPECTED DREAM

***

Skylar Donohue stood nervously in the dugout. She chewed on the inside of her cheek, not wanting to move to grab more sunflower seeds because she might miss the moment they won the game. She never counted her chickens, so to speak. They could still lose. She'd watched team after team get a big lead going into the final inning, only to lose it and then lose the game itself. It had happened to her more times than she could count as a player, and now, as a first-time pitching coach, she was just hoping it wouldn't happen today.

Today was too important. The sport had just been added back, and the US team and federation had worked so hard to get it included again. She wanted to be part of the reason they brought home the gold medal. If she couldn't do it as a pitcher, because of some wrist injury, she would do it as a pitching coach.

"What do you think?" the head coach asked her.

"Fastball. She's not hitting the spots with her change-up right now. Two-seam fastball and then a screwball. That's been working well for her with this hitter," Skylar replied.

"Give the signal, coach."

Skylar nodded toward the catcher. She gave her the signal for the fastball, and the catcher relayed the signal to the pitcher. Then, Skylar waited. When the game would end, she'd hate herself a little bit because no matter the outcome today, she wasn't playing. Coaches didn't get medals; only the players did. And Skylar had a long road to recovery if she was ever going to get to wear one of the gold ones around her neck.

Later that night, Skylar scrolled through the ESPN app on her phone. She couldn't sleep, and she also knew she wouldn't be able to for a while. Checking scores and watching some highlight videos sometimes helped her wind down, oddly enough. Before she could get to the scores tab, though, she noticed a two-minute video of Wyatt Wicked, the volleyball superstar who had just won the gold medal for the US the day before.

"This is another important victory for this team. Bringing home this gold will help solidify the pro league we've been working hard to build for years. We're hoping a victory tour, celebrating our win in Tokyo, will bring even more attention to the sport. We want to continue to develop our homegrown talent, build an academy and clinics, and work with young women who dream of having one of these around their neck one day." Wyatt held up the gold medal and smiled widely.

"You also just got engaged, surprising everyone. What's better? Winning this medal, or proposing to your girlfriend and her saying yes?"

Wyatt chuckled, and Skylar could see why people found her charming. She *was* charming. She was gorgeous, talented, and one of the hardest workers Skylar had seen or, at least, heard about, since she had only met Wyatt twice and mainly in passing.

"This means a lot to me." The woman looked down at the medal. *"I've worked my entire life for this moment, and so have the other women who stood up on the podium with me. But Everly is my heart, and I love her like I've never loved anyone before. I can't wait to marry her, and both of these amazing things happening to me in one day is pretty overwhelming."*

Skylar liked the non-answer. The reporter asked Wyatt another question. Then, the interview was over. Skylar went to the scores tab of the app and began searching for the other Olympic events she'd missed as she'd been focusing on her own. It was then that she wondered if she'd ever have the chance to do what Wyatt had done. She wanted to be part of a pro softball league in the States. Maybe now that the sport had been added back, and they had done so well today, she would have that chance.

CHAPTER 1

"I CANNOT believe it's taken this long," Mia said.

"Divorce cases when custody agreements are involved sometimes do. In this case, your soon to be ex-husband hasn't exactly made things easy on us," her lawyer replied.

"He doesn't even want custody," Mia said. "He's using our daughter to make things difficult for me."

"It doesn't matter. We'll have everything wrapped up today. He's agreed to it all, finally. He just needs to sign. Then, you sign, and we'll file the paperwork."

"What if he refuses again?"

"I doubt he will. He asked for weekend visits. When we countered with every other weekend just to see what he'd say, he agreed and even suggested once a month because he travels a lot for work. He didn't even ask for holidays or something during the summer, when she's out of school."

"She's two years old," Mia said.

"But these agreements are binding until she's eighteen unless you go back to court to make changes or agree to something on your own, so we had to include it. He didn't press when I said you could alternate holidays."

"He has a new girlfriend," Mia stated. "She's twenty-two years old."

"You're not exactly much older than that, Mia," her lawyer replied, nodding at her.

"I hit thirty this year."

"I'm forty-five. What must he think of *me*?" She laughed at her own joke.

The door to the conference room opened, and her ex-husband, Gregg, and his lawyer entered the space with the small round conference table. The room looked sterile. It had the dark brown table in the middle with six rather uncomfortable chairs around it. There was a clear pitcher of water and six glasses on a tray in the middle of the table. There were also two filing cabinets in the corner, and Mia hoped her case and information wasn't inside the one on the left because one of the drawers was open.

"Mia," Gregg greeted.

"Hi, Gregg," she replied, giving him a forced smile.

"My client has agreed to the terms of the custody agreement. However, he'd like to make one–"

"No, Don," Mia's lawyer interjected. "No more concessions on my client's part. We agreed we're ready to sign. This has dragged on long enough. We're here to sign these papers."

"My client would like some assurances that when your client begins a new relationship, which she will likely do at some point, that–"

"New relationship? I'm not even dating. I have a two-year-old child and a full-time job. When would I–"

"Mia, it's okay." Her lawyer placed a hand on top of her own.

Gregg looked down at their hands; they were not joined or intertwined, but it obviously made him feel uncomfortable.

"Are you sure you're not dating?" Gregg asked, nodding toward the hands.

"She's my attorney, Gregg!" Mia practically spat out.

"Mr. Landis, my client's future relationships – whatever and whenever they may be, and whomever they might be with – is of none of your concern."

"It will be if she brings someone home and my daughter is there," he replied.

"Gregg, where is this coming from?" Mia asked.

"You could bring a woman home. What kind of–"

"*You* left me," she interrupted. "You couldn't deal with–"

"Mia, please." Her attorney turned toward her a bit. "Don, this relationship gambit is off the table. Your client has a financial obligation to his daughter. Outside of that, he has monthly weekend visits, alternate holidays, and this was all agreed upon already. If he chooses to, he can terminate his parental rights and have none of those things."

"Terminate my rights?"

"You didn't want her to begin with, Gregg," Mia reminded him. "When I got pregnant, you already had one foot out the door."

"And if you press this relationship thing further, Don, we'll go in front of the judge, and I'll bring up your client's infidelity before and *after* he found out his wife was pregnant."

"That was only after she told me–"

"Mr. Landis, this is the deal," Mia's attorney interrupted again. "Sign the divorce papers today so that you can move on with your life and Mia can move on with hers."

"Let me confer with my client," Don said, leaning over and whispering something into Gregg's ear.

After a moment, he stopped and turned back to the table. Mia wiped her hands over her black pants. The only thing she wanted was her daughter. It wasn't like they had any real money between them. They had the house, but she'd left that to Gregg and hadn't argued about it in the settlement. They each had their own cars, so there was no need to figure that out. Mia had moved into a two-bedroom apartment close to the high school where she worked, and that should have been the end of it. Gregg had initiated the separation and, later, the divorce proceedings. It had been over a year of this back and forth, and Mia was running out of money. It wasn't like her job paid well, and the court fees and attorney fees were piling up because Gregg was dragging this out to soothe his own injured ego, and that was driving her crazy.

"Fine," he finally said. "Let's just do this so that I can get back to work."

Mia resisted the urge to argue further. She had a job, too, after all. She hadn't ever planned to get married. She definitely hadn't planned on getting divorced. So much had happened; so much has changed in her life since she had met Gregg at the age of twenty-one while they were both student-athletes in college. It was now nine years later, and she was signing divorce papers.

At least, the whole thing was over now. Mia thanked her lawyer and climbed into her car. A moment later, she finally let out the sigh of relief she had been holding in for years. She was divorced. Well, she would be as soon as everything was filed and processed; but for all intents and purposes, she was now a single woman. She was a single parent. Mia closed her eyes and leaned her head against the back of the seat. She knew Gregg wouldn't be reliable as a father. She hated to think that way, but Gregg hadn't ever wanted children.

When Mia had mentioned that she had changed her mind on that topic and wanted to talk further about them having children, he had groaned. She wasn't certain, but it might have been around that time that Gregg started to stray. Hazel wasn't planned. Mia would never in a million years regret having her daughter, but the fact that she had been an accident, and that Gregg and Mia were both thinking about getting out of their marriage, had made the pregnancy and the first two years of her young daughter's life a little more complicated than she had hoped. Hazel hadn't noticed, and that was the important thing. Mia only had one focus now that the papers were signed. She was going to give Hazel the best life she could, surrounding the girl with people who loved her, and she silently hoped that Gregg would actually decide to step up to the plate and be a real father to his daughter.

***

"How did it go today?" Rhodes asked her.

"It's done," Mia replied, placing her bag in the dugout.

"Really? That's fantastic," Rhodes said. "It is fantastic, right? I don't know what to say to someone who just got divorced, but it's something she's wanted."

"It's a good thing," Mia replied as she pulled her long blonde hair back into the requisite ponytail and slid her dark blue hat onto her head, pulling her hair through the hole in the back. "I'm ready for it to be over."

"Don't take this the wrong way, but Gregg is an ass. What did you ever see in him?"

Mia sighed, turned toward the field to watch the girls warming up, and said, "Honestly, I look back now, and I have no idea. But when we first met, it made perfect sense. He was the reluctant college soccer star. I was the prodigy pitcher who had just gotten called up to the national team. We met in class and talked about how it wasn't easy to keep up with school and the sport. He was a nice guy who treated me well back then."

"What happened then?" she asked.

"Rhodes, if I knew, I'd tell you. But I think we fell out of love a long time ago. He made the MLS out of school. We moved and got married shortly after. Then, he got traded and traded, and finally, he got cut. He was twenty-five and had no idea what he wanted to do with his life."

"And you were kicking ass on the national team," Rhodes said.

"It didn't exactly matter, though, did it? We weren't going anywhere on the big stage with no Olympics. I guess he just felt lost and didn't want to admit it. I went through years of that, thinking this is what you sign up for in marriage. For better or worse, right?"

"That's what they say, but I wouldn't know." Rhodes looked out at the field. "Do you want to continue this conversation after practice? I'll buy the first round."

"I have to pick Hazel up from my mom's, but thanks for the offer," Mia replied.

"Offer's open if you want."

"Thanks, Rhodes," she said, turning to smile at the woman. "I'll grab the pitchers and catchers to get them on drills."

"I'll take the infielders and let Stan handle the outfielders. I want a pretty chill practice today. We don't need any injuries or tired arms. Let's have some fun and keep them lose. Playoffs are a big deal around here."

"Don't I know it," Mia stated, laughing a little as she headed out to the field.

She *did* know that. This was her old high school. She had spent some of the best years of her life on this field, playing ball. They'd been state champions three out of her four years here. Since she had left, they'd only won one more championship. This year, Mia hoped to take them back to the championship and bring that trophy home to her alma mater. She had been bouncing from school to school as an assistant coach for the past three years. The spot opened up here only a few months prior to work with Rhodes, who had been the assistant here when Mia was a student. Shortly after joining as the assistant coach, the PE teacher retired, and Mia, who had majored in kinesiology in school – as a lot of student-athletes did, was able to apply and scoop up the job. It meant she would have more money, but it also meant she'd be at work all day, five days a week, and then on the weekends, there were games and practices.

Her mom, who had recently retired early due to a workplace fall, was her go-to babysitter. The woman loved being a grandma and didn't charge anything – which was great given Mia's current financial situation, but she didn't like using her mom for babysitting services, especially since she still hadn't fully recovered from her injury. It was the best she could do for now, though.

Practice was a fun one. The girls were excited to begin the playoffs as the only undefeated team in the state. The team was filled with seniors who had been in the championship game the previous season, where they had lost by only one run. There were three juniors who had been on the junior varsity squad, and one amazing sophomore that Mia worked with most days since she had been a pitcher, and this sixteen-year-old girl was one fantastic pitcher. Mia could see her making the national squad before the Paris games and could easily see her going to a softball college and winning national championships for her school.

"You're releasing a little too early on your fastball," Mia told her as they walked to the parking lot after practice.

"It's been slipping more than normal," the girl replied.

"You need to chalk more," Mia said. "If it's slipping when you release, chalk with every pitch. I used to rub the inside of my glove with chalk. Pound the chalk bag into it. When you're pulling back, slide your fingers around in the pocket of the glove. Then, grip the ball."

"Why don't I just use the bag?"

"You can, but you don't use it for your other pitches. You go out at the beginning of the inning, grab it, bounce it a bit, and that's all you do with it until the next inning. If you use it more, just make sure it's not with *just* the fastball. They'll be able to tell pretty quickly."

"True," the girl replied. "Hey, thanks."

"That's what I'm here for," Mia said, smiling over at her.

"Not every high school student gets to be trained by an Olympian, though," she replied.

"I think that's a common misconception," Mia began. "I never went to the Olympics."

"You were on the national team, though. That counts."

"Not as much as you'd think." Mia sighed.

"Hey, I meant to ask you something. Do you have a minute?"

"Sure."

They stopped in front of Mia's car.

"So, my parents got this call from someone saying they were a part of this new pro league in the States. I guess they're trying to start something here, and they wanted to know if I'd be interested in playing in it after I graduate."

"Wait… A new pro softball league?" Mia checked.

"Yeah. I looked it up online. It's the real deal. They've been working on it for a few years, I guess. It's like eight teams to start. Anyway, they're thinking about creating some kind of an academy for potential players, and they invited me to their summer clinic. It's basically a try-out. If I make it through, I'd participate with one of their academy teams in tournaments and stuff. Then, when I get out of high school, I could join the real league."

"High school? What about college?" Mia asked.

"I guess I'd have to make that choice. I can't go pro and play in the NCAA."

"College. You should go to college."

"I know. I know you're right, but you've been in my shoes. You were a pitcher, and people scouted you. If this were you, would you at least go this summer?"

"Absolutely," Mia advised. "You have travel ball this summer, but you can skip that for this; and you should. If they think this pro league is going to last, this is a great opportunity for you. I just don't want you to skip college. Softball isn't the only thing in the world, and if you don't get a degree, that's going to bite you later. Plus, no matter how much they pay these players, it's not going to be NFL or NBA money, so you need a fallback and, possibly, even a part-time job to supplement."

"Oh, I guess," the girl said, looking down at the loose gravel beneath her feet.

That was when Mia remembered she was only a sixteen-year-old girl and probably not at all interested in hearing about the downsides right now.

"Hey, this is amazing news. I am very proud of you. And I'm happy to talk to your parents about any of this, but right now, I need your head in the playoffs. Can you do that?"

"No problem," the girl said with a smile. "Hey, what about you?"

"What about me?" Mia asked just as she opened her car door.

"Are you going to join?"

"Join what?"

"The league." She chuckled. "They're having open try-outs in a bunch of cities starting in a couple of weeks. I can send you the link."

"Why?"

"Because you could try out."

"Oh, my playing days are over. I have a daughter, and I'm–"

"Still a kick-ass pitcher," the girl interrupted. "You should think about it, coach."

CHAPTER 2

"PLEASE tell me I'm good to go," Skylar said.

"Skylar, it's okay, but you could use another month or two of rehab," the physical therapist replied.

"It was an outpatient procedure," she said.

"Yes, but I know you know about all the tiny bones, tendons, and nerves in the wrist. You know it's not that simple. Maybe if you weren't an athlete, it would be fine. You could wear a brace or something. But if you're trying to get back into playing, you should take another couple of months to rehab it first."

"I don't have a couple of months. The try-out is in thirteen days."

"Skylar, your wrist needs more time."

"It's fine when I catch," she said.

"No, it's not ready for you to catch fastballs from Olympians, but you do it anyway."

"You said I couldn't pitch anymore," Skylar said.

"I did."

"Well, I caught before high school, and when I had a bad shoulder my junior year of high school, I spent the whole season behind the plate. I actually got scouted as a catcher before they knew I could pitch. I've been practicing a little with the team, and it doesn't hurt my wrist like it does when I pitch."

"That's because you're not using it as much as when you pitch. It's the repetitive motion that caused you so many problems. When you get it back to the pitcher, it's a toss.

14

It's not a fastball that requires you to hold the ball a certain way or snap your wrist so directly and quickly." The physical therapist walked over to Skylar and began massaging her wrist a bit. "Does this hurt?"

Skylar winced internally and said, "No."

"Sky, we've known each other for years. You can't lie to me."

"It hurts a little, but not as much as last week," Skylar replied honestly.

"You know that if you rehab this the right way, you could be stronger and better next year, right?"

"It's the first year of the league. I have to be a part of that if I can," Skylar replied, pulling her wrist back and rubbing it. "Besides, it's a try-out because it's the first year, but next year, they'll have a draft. They'll be going after college students. I'm not in college. This is important."

"So is your job as a coach on this team. If you play professionally, you know you can't coach the national team, too. If the league crashes or if you end up hurt worse than you are now, they'll have already found your replacement here. You understand that, right?"

"What can I say? I've always been a risk-taker." She shrugged.

Skylar left the physical therapy office a few minutes later. She knew the doctor and everyone else she'd consulted about her injury was right. She should continue to rest it, wear the brace she had been given, and wait until it was fully healed. She also knew that pro league try-outs were in less than two weeks, and she had no intention of missing them. She had dreamed of becoming a professional softball player as a kid, growing up in a small Midwest town. She hadn't had much as a kid. Money wasn't exactly plentiful in her house. God was the main topic of conversation most days, but that hadn't bothered her much. It was just the way her family was; always talking about Christ, and faith, and going to church. It had never been her thing, but she'd respected her parents and went along with it when she had to.

Softball had been her thing. She started playing baseball because her two older brothers did, and if she played baseball, her parents could go to one place, drop them all off for practice or games, and come back later. After tee-ball, though, she moved to softball because her oldest brother, Sal Jr., had gotten his driver's license and could take her on his way to practice with her other brother Steven, who was fourteen. She'd chosen to play catcher because the gear looked cool. That was the reason. She had been eight years old at the time and thought the mask looked interesting. Skylar liked being behind the plate, but she really liked being *at* the plate. She loved hitting, and she'd been good at it.

At first, she had only played during the summers, but by the time she was twelve, her church had sponsored her travel ball and fall league. She even played indoor in the harsh Midwest winters. At fourteen, her coach thought she might have a good arm. They had needed a pitcher, so she had given it a try. She had been good; good enough to start for her high school team at the varsity level that year. There was that junior year season behind the plate, but after that, she had only pitched. After four years in college and a couple of championships, Skylar had planned to join the national team. She pitched in a try-out and did well. During the try-out, she had been running from second to third after a teammate smacked a line drive off the bat. It would have been an easy base hit, except Skylar had been running in its path. The ball smacked right into her wrist. She'd finished the try-out despite the pain and the swelling, choosing not to show the team doctors. When she got to her hotel later that night, she self-medicated with Ibuprofen and ice, hoping it would go down. It didn't.

She had the first operation shortly after. That had taken her out of the running as a player, but the coaching staff had been impressed with her and asked if she wanted to be an assistant on the team. She'd accepted and rehabbed her wrist in their facilities, wanting to keep as close to the team as possible because there would be a moment when her wrist would be fine, and she wanted to be there when that happened. Skylar had never planned on being twenty-five years old and coaching, but after a year of being an assistant, she had been promoted to work with the pitchers a year prior; only ten weeks before the Olympics. She could continue on as a coach, but she couldn't let go of the fact that she was only twenty-five. She had years of playing left in her. She had kept in shape. She had kept up on the game. She just needed her damn wrist to heal, and she could play in this pro league and maybe even at the national level for Paris. She had had the second, less serious operation not that long ago, to take care of some scar tissue, and while it was still hurting, it wasn't nearly as bad as it had been. She considered that a victory.

When she got home, she iced her wrist for twenty minutes per doctor's instructions and then put it in the brace. She had been crossing the line a little by practicing with the players, but she trusted herself and would stop when she felt the pain coming on. Today, she hadn't practiced with the team. She had kept the brace on at all times outside of her appointment and had taken the Ibuprofen as recommended. She was doing everything she could to get back to playing. She would be ready in thirteen days.

"Hey, babe," Tori greeted.

"Hey," Skylar replied.

"You sound happy. How was PT?"

"Fine," she said as Tori walked into her apartment, using the key Skylar had given her a year ago.

"Fine, huh?" Tori checked, flopping down next to her on the sofa.

"Can you at least change before you sit down?" Skylar asked her, only half-joking. "Did you have sliding practice today or something? You're filthy."

"We did do base running drills, yes, Sky." The woman smiled and then rolled her eyes. "But after that, it started

17

raining, so we all had fun in the mud."

"Fun in the mud?"

"Yes, I know you remember what that's like. You're not *that* old," Tori teased, kissed Skylar on the cheek, and then stood up.

"I'm only three years older than you," Skylar said.

"Then, stop acting like a grandma. I'm hopping in the shower. Do you want to go out for dinner?"

"No, I was thinking about ordering in, actually," Skylar replied.

"Really? I wanted to go out. I thought we could hit up Jake's Tavern after. A couple of the girls are going to be there," she said, removing her dirty t-shirt.

"I'd rather stay in, Tor. Can we do something with them this weekend?" she asked.

"Beth's boyfriend is in town this week. He heads back on Friday. She wants us to meet him."

"Why?" Skylar asked, watching as Tori removed her sports bra.

"Because she's a teammate and one of my closest friends, and I've never met him."

"She's a freshman, Tor. Let me guess. This is the high school boyfriend she's trying to make it last with now that she's in college?"

Tori paused her hands on her pants and asked, "God, when did you get so cynical?"

"I'm not cynical."

"Yeah, you are. Who cares if they last or not? They're together now. She loves him, and she wants me to meet him. I told her we'd go tonight."

"Why don't you go? I'm tired, and my wrist hurts from PT."

Tori slid off her pants and said, "Fine." She then sighed audibly. "Are you okay?"

"I just told you—"

"I mean, in general. You seem upset."

"I'm not upset, Tor."

"I don't just mean tonight."

"Tori, you're basically naked. Take your shower. We can talk about this later."

"I came over here to have dinner with my girlfriend, not just to borrow your shower, Sky." Tori slid the dirty shirt back over her head and walked back to the sofa, wearing that and her underwear. "Are you nervous about the whole meet the parents thing?"

"What? No."

"Really? *I* would be if you ever introduced me to your parents," she said, sitting back down.

"My parents refer to you as *that girl* and asked me just last week if I went to church. And two weeks ago, they asked if I'd met a nice man. They've visited me here exactly zero times, and I only go back for major holidays when I have to."

"Well, *my* parents are coming to town for senior night, and they want to meet my girlfriend of almost two years." She kissed Skylar's cheek. "That's okay, right?"

"Yeah, sure," Skylar replied.

"You sound *so* excited about it," Tori replied sarcastically.

"Am I supposed to be excited about meeting your parents? That's not generally something people get excited about."

"It's a big step in our relationship, Sky. I think it's a pretty big one. You know I'm about to graduate."

"Yes, I know that."

"I've been living in the athletic dorm for four years. I'm ready to move out."

"That's generally what happens when—"

"Skylar, are you even listening to me?" the woman interrupted.

"Yes, I'm listening. What—"

"We've been together for two years. You honestly haven't thought about what would happen after I graduated?"

"I thought you'd get an apartment."

"You don't want to move in together?" Tori asked.

"Tor, the last time we talked about this, you said you wanted to get an apartment on your own. It was important to you, so I didn't press."

"That was six months ago. A lot has changed since then."

"Has it?" Skylar asked, standing up to get something to drink from her kitchen.

"What's that supposed to mean?"

"Nothing. I'm sorry. I'm tired. I think I'm going to just eat a TV dinner or something and crash."

"You've been acting weird lately."

"I have not."

"Is this about the league thing?"

"The league thing?" Skylar asked, turning back to Tori. "The league thing is a pretty important deal, Tori."

"I know it is." She shrugged. "I get it."

"Do you?"

"I know your wrist has been hurting, but you're still planning to try out."

"Because it's my dream. You play softball in college, but you want to be a pharmacist. I've only ever wanted to play this sport."

"So, because I play in college but never thought about going pro at something, it's less of a big deal?"

"That's not what I'm saying."

"They called me yesterday, you know?"

"Who did?"

"The league, or whoever they had scouting talent. They called a bunch of university seniors at the so-called softball schools. They asked me to try out."

"They asked you to try out?" Skylar asked, moving back toward the sofa.

"Yeah, is that so hard to imagine? I know we had a shitty season this year, and we're not making the playoffs, but *I'm* good. They wanted me to try out now that I'm graduating and can go pro."

"You want to be a pharmacist," Skylar said as she sat back down next to her.

"I do, but I also love softball, Sky. I'm twenty-two. I can play for a few years, at least. If this league takes off, I can play for however long I want and have pharmacy right there waiting. I can even go to grad school online if I want."

"So, you're doing it?"

"Trying out? I don't know. I was going to talk to you about it first. I mean, we don't play the same position, so it's not like we're in competition or anything, but I know how important this is to you, so I wanted to talk."

"If you want to do it, you should do it." Skylar looked away from Tori.

"It bugs you, doesn't it?"

"What?"

"That they called me," she said. "That I'm able to play and possibly make one of the teams."

"No. Why would it?"

"Because it's your dream, not mine. You were on track to play in the Olympics, and I've never cared about that. I just love the sport. Now, I'm on track for something like that."

"Are you asking if I'm jealous?"

"I'm trying to find a reason why you've been pulling away lately."

"I haven't been pulling away, Tori. We're just in different places in our lives."

"Now we're in different places… But just two nights ago, we were fucking in your bedroom, and you were telling me you loved me."

"Tor—"

"No, tell me about this place you're in, and why I'm not there."

"I don't know. I've been feeling that way a lot lately," Skylar replied, leaning back against the sofa. "You haven't noticed?"

"That I love you? I've noticed that," Tori said, placing a hand on Skylar's knee. "I love you, Sky. I have since we met at that slow pitch league championship you coached and I played on the other team. I think I fell in love with you when you threw your drink at that guy who was hitting on you, turned around, saw me laughing, and took me by the hand–"

"Outside. I remember," Skylar said with a soft smile.

"We had our first date that next night." Tori smiled then. "I've loved you since."

"I know. Me too," Skylar replied.

"Then, what's going on?"

"You want to go out, Tor. You have finals. You have a senior night."

"You did those things, too," Tori said.

"I *did* those things. I don't anymore."

"I can't help that I'm in college, Sky. You knew exactly how old I was when you met me."

"I know."

"Is this a problem? I'm about to graduate, babe."

"I know," Skylar said again. "I don't know what's going on with me. I'm sorry. It's not your fault. I just have a lot to think about."

"Am I one of those things?" Tori pulled her hand away from Skylar's knee.

"No." Skylar shook her head and then stopped. "I don't know."

"My parents are coming to town for two reasons, Skylar. They want to watch me play a game they've seen me play a thousand times before, and they want to meet my girlfriend for the first time because I told them that this thing with us was real; that we were moving in together soon. I told them you and I wanted the same things. Is that not true anymore?"

Skylar turned to look at her and said, "I don't know."

CHAPTER 3

"EIGHT teams?" Rhodes asked.

"Yeah. I don't know. It's crazy, right? I've got a two-year-old at home and a job," Mia said.

"And a dream," Rhodes replied. "You love the sport. It's why you're coaching. You were close to going to Tokyo, but you had Hazel. If you join this league, it'll bring some focus back on you and give you a shot at Paris."

"I'm thirty years old, Rhodes. Paris is three years away."

"Softball doesn't attack the body like some other sports. You've kept in shape enough. You just need to test your arm a bit and see if it's ready to pitch again."

"And if it is?"

"As your boss, I say, do nothing." Rhodes winked at her. "As your friend, I say, go for it. You don't exactly have anything to lose. If you don't make it, you're still an assistant coach at your alma mater. You're still about to help us get back to the state championship. If you make it, you get to play the sport you love and make money doing it. You'd have a chance of getting back on the national team, and you could be winning a medal in 2024."

"Let's not get ahead of ourselves," she replied.

"Plenty of women do this stuff with kids, Mia."

"How many of them are single parents?"

"I don't know the exact numbers, but I'm sure there are many." Rhodes paused and looked over at Hazel, who was playing with her toys on the living room floor. "Has Gregg not had a visit yet?"

"His first official visit, after we signed the papers, was supposed to be this weekend. He called to cancel this morning."

"Did he give a reason?"

"He didn't have to. He never wanted her." Mia smiled at her adorable daughter. "He used her to make sure I would give him the house and not press for alimony."

"You didn't?"

"No. I only want child support for her. He'll pay that. I doubt he'll visit often or do much actual fathering beyond that."

"All because he couldn't handle you being bisexual?" Rhodes asked, taking a drink of her beer.

"I think if I had realized it earlier, he either wouldn't have dated me when I told him, or he would have adjusted to it before we got married."

"I just don't get that."

"I honestly didn't know I was attracted to women as well. I've been around naked women in locker rooms before. I've had close friends. I never thought about dating any of them. Then, I met Francesca."

"Because, of course, her name is Francesca." Rhodes laughed.

Mia laughed back and said, "I know. But it was like I'd been missing something with Gregg, you know? It didn't have to do with him being a man or her being a woman. It was just who she was as a person. I was totally into her in a way I had never been into Gregg. She wanted a wife and kids and, coincidentally enough, had played softball as a kid. Gregg only went to my games in school because he had no excuse."

"I will still never understand why you–"

"I know." Mia laughed again. "I'm an idiot. I get it."

"Can I ask something I've never asked you?"

"You want to know if I cheated on him," she stated.

"Yeah, I guess that's what I'm asking."

"No, I didn't. But once we were separated legally, and I knew he couldn't punish me in the divorce papers, I went out a few times and felt like getting revenge. He'd been cheating for a while, so I thought it was my turn to sleep with other people."

"How'd *that* go?"

"It wasn't a good phase, but I blew off some steam, and then I knew for sure that it wasn't about Gregg or Francesca. I like men *and* women."

"Some people don't get how that can be."

"I know. Gregg is one of them. When Francesca and I started hanging out, that's when I told him. I'd been out with her. We had had a few drinks at a bar, and I was a little tipsy. He was upset I had been out so late. I was stupid and thought that was the right time to tell my husband that I thought I was attracted to women." Mia laughed at herself. "He told me he didn't want me to hang out with her anymore. I told him he couldn't tell me who I could be friends with."

"And you still stayed with him?"

"He apologized the next day. We talked for a while about what it meant to me; for us. I told him we were married, and me being attracted to women didn't change that. Then, sometime later, I got pregnant. I think that was the last straw. He didn't like that I was still spending time with Francesca. He didn't know for sure that I had feelings for her. I never confessed to that, but I think he figured it out. When we found out about Hazel, that was it. That was the end of our marriage."

"Mama," Hazel said.

"Yes, baby?"

"Look." Hazel held up two dolls.

"Pretty," Mia replied, not sure what she was supposed to say about the two dolls that looked exactly the same as when she had placed them in front of her daughter.

Hazel smiled and turned back around to continue playing.

"You know what I think?" Rhodes asked before she finished her beer.

"What?"

"I think that you should try out. You have a rocket for an arm, and you have the softball IQ. Just go and see what happens. If you don't make it, you don't make it. But that little girl right there is going to have big dreams of her own one day. I think you owe it to her to at least try one last time to make your own come true. That's a pretty important lesson; don't you think?"

***

"Mom, are you sure you're okay with this?" Mia asked.

"We'll be fine," her mother replied, taking Hazel from her arms. "It's only five days. I had you for eighteen years, didn't I?"

"She's my responsibility, Mom," Mia reminded, passing Hazel's bag to her mother.

"Every parent needs a babysitter, Mia. I happen to enjoy spending time with my granddaughter. You go, do what you need to do. We'll be here when you get back."

"Am I crazy? I left the team when Gregg and I started having problems. I planned to go back, but then I got pregnant. I think they've forgotten about me."

"You left the national team. This isn't the national team, Mia. This is an entirely new league that you could be a part of. If it works out, maybe the national team will come calling again. But if none of this happens, I don't think you're crazy for following your dream. I think you'd be crazy not to."

"We're in the middle of the playoffs," Mia said.

"Are you trying to come up with excuses not to go?"

"No, I'm *not* trying. They're just there. We have three games left. I'm leaving for five days of important practices. What if I come back and we lose?"

"Are you pitching in the game? Are you hitting? Your team will be fine. They're in good hands, and they will prepare themselves without you. Rhodes gave you the time off, didn't she?"

"Yes, and the school actually thought it would be a good publicity thing if I tried out, even if I don't make a team. They're spinning this as *the hometown girl done good* and plan to have the news interview me before the next game."

"High school has changed since I was a student," her mother said. "Say goodbye to your mama, Hazel."

Mia said goodbye to her daughter, which she hated doing. Then, she turned around and got into the car. She had had to put the flight on her one credit card that wasn't maxed out, because they didn't have try-outs near enough for her to drive. This was crazy. People weren't telling her that, but it was crazy. She wasn't going to make a team. She would have to return home defeated and try to play it off like it wasn't a big deal, when it was to her. She could do that, though. The girls on the team would need her to do that, and Hazel would get to know one day about how her mom didn't quit when there was something she wanted. So, no matter what happened, that would make it worth it.

***

Mia checked into the hotel that she also put on that credit card, and hurried off to her room. She needed a bathroom. The drive from the airport in her rental had been a long one. She had gotten turned around a few times and, as a result, needed to get to the bathroom quickly. When she opened the door to the room, she rushed inside the bathroom, knelt in front of the toilet, and promptly vomited. What the hell had she been thinking? She had needed to pee about an hour into her drive, but she hadn't expected on vomiting. When she'd walked into the hotel, the closest one in town to the location of the try-outs, she saw about thirty young women milling about, carrying bat bags and other luggage over their shoulders and wearing shirts, sweatpants, and hats – all emblazoned with their university logos.

Yeah, she'd been nuts to think she had a chance of making one of eight teams. For the Olympics, there were usually eighteen players on the roster, with a bunch of alternates waiting in the wings for their shot at joining. In this league, they were fielding teams of twenty-three players to start, in case of injury. That meant that every position would have a backup, and likely, they'd have an extra catcher, maybe a power hitter that wasn't the best at defense, and the rest would all be pitchers.

Mia cleaned herself up and took a shower. She then climbed into bed, still with wet hair, and called her mom to talk to Hazel before she went to sleep. Tomorrow was the first day of the try-out. They would be cutting players at the end of each day, so Mia had kept her flight back home open as a result. She expected to be home tomorrow night or the following morning, at the latest, but she also told herself she would go out there and give it all she had. She owed it to herself to do that.

CHAPTER 4

SKYLAR stood on the field as a player for the first time in a long time. Her wrist felt fine. It wasn't healed all the way, but it felt better than it had since the second surgery. She had had it wrapped to reduce the strain from the try-out, and it was a little too tight, but she could still bend it when she needed to. There were at least one hundred women out here today. This was one of ten regional try-out locations. Skylar expected that some of them would have even more than a hundred women. That meant at least one thousand women were vying for one hundred and eighty-four slots. The odds weren't in her favor, but then again, they weren't really in anyone else's favor, either.

"Welcome to the try-out for the future Women's Professional Fastpitch Softball League," one of the coaches said to the group that was sitting in the middle of the outfield. "Most of you know, we've attempted professional leagues in the US before. We've had some limited success, but this is the first time we've had the backing, the money, and the timing to launch something at this scale. There are eight teams that will play a shortened summer season. Think of it as an exhibition season. It's a warm-up round. Next spring, we launch in earnest, with a full season and twenty-three players on each team. The cities chosen for the league are Cincinnati, Chicago, Orlando, Houston, Las Vegas, Oklahoma City, Providence, and Boise. If you are chosen for a team, you will be told at the end of this week which one that would be. You'll have two weeks to report to your first practice. Small relocation stipends will be provided, but you'll ultimately need to decide if moving to one of these cities is something you can and will do. If not, we will have alternate selections at the ready. There is no trade window this year. The team you're on is the team you're on. Everyone understand?"

There was a shout of yes from the women sitting down.

"All right. Let's go over the plan for the day. We have position coaches that will break you into your groups. They'll be making their observations and notes throughout the day. At the end of the day, we'll be cutting the players we won't be inviting back for tomorrow. Tonight, the coaches will all connect across the country and see where we are. We'll do the same thing each day for the next five days to get us down to the one hundred and eighty-four players we need, along with twenty alternates. If you're an alternate, we'll let you know the next steps at that time. Now, we've got a lot of work ahead of us this week. Let's get everyone broken up. Outfielders, stay here. If you're first base, head toward first. Second base, do the same at second. I'll take third and short to batting practice. Pitchers and catchers head to the bullpen."

"Are you ready?" Tori asked her as she stood up.

"I don't have a choice, do I?" Skylar replied.

"Sky, come on. Don't be like that. I know things are off with us right now, but–"

"No, that's not what I meant. I'm sorry," Skylar interrupted and stood up herself. "It's just that this might be my last shot at this. That's what I meant. I have to be ready."

"You've got this, okay? Don't go crazy. You just need to make a couple of good throw downs today, swing the bat a bit, and you'll make it to tomorrow. Then, you can see how your wrist does."

"Yeah," Skylar said.

"I'd kiss you, but we're technically at work." Tori walked off toward the outfielders.

Skylar headed toward the bullpen, where she noticed ten pitchers and five women with their own catcher's gear waiting already. She just needed to be better than at least one of them today. She had no idea if that was good enough, but that was what she'd tell herself to help diminish her nerves. It wasn't helping that Tori was here. Things had been tense between them over the past couple of weeks. Skylar had met her parents reluctantly, since she thought they still had a lot to talk through before taking that step. Tori's parents seemed to like her enough but did ask her what she planned to do with her life now that she wasn't playing. She supposed they wanted to know if she would coach forever or if she had something else in her. Truthfully, it was a fair question. She just didn't know that herself yet.

Tori was her first serious girlfriend after a few short-term things in college. They had been pretty hot and heavy for their first year together. Then, Skylar had given her a key to her place, and she thought they would be together for the long haul, but Tori was young. The three years between them weren't that big of a deal, but what Skylar had discovered was that her injury had aged her mentally and emotionally, and although Tori had been there to support her through it all, it wasn't the same as it had been. Skylar had been thinking about ending things between them for the past month or so, but she hadn't had the guts. Now, she had to focus on playing the sport she loved at a level that would earn her a spot in tomorrow's try-out. She couldn't and wouldn't think or worry about whatever Tori was doing today, and she knew Tori wouldn't be worried or thinking about her.

***

Hours later, her wrist was hurting, but she was hanging in there. She had spent three hours behind the plate, which was a big difference from standing on the mound. Her knees were killing her, and she knew she would be icing them later at home. She'd held her own, though. Then, batting practice had presented some wrist challenges, but Skylar had managed some good swings. They did some conditioning, which she excelled at because she always kept herself in game-ready shape. When the first day was over, they had all the players sit in the bleachers. The coaches went into the opposite dugout and had a long conversation as the women took off their cleats and tucked their gear into their bags. They talked to one another about how the first day had gone and where they hoped to end up if they made it.

"Hey, can I come to your place tonight?" Tori asked.

"Aren't you moving out of the dorm tomorrow?" Skylar asked.

"Yes. Why?"

"You don't want to spend your last night in college in the dorm?" Skylar asked, sliding off her dirty shoe.

"Not really. I'd like to spend the night with my girlfriend, who's been avoiding me for the past few days."

"I'm trying to focus on this, Tor." She motioned with her hand to the field.

"So, you can't focus on us and this at the same time?"

"Not really, no."

"Meredith let me take the extra bedroom in her new place because her other roommate backed out when she got into grad school at Wisconsin. That's the only reason I have a place to live, Sky. Does that matter to you?"

"Does it matter to you that you just assumed you were moving in with me, even though we hadn't talked about it in six months?" Skylar asked her.

"Ladies, we have posted the cut list to the dugout

wall," one of the coaches announced as he walked toward the bleachers. "If your name is on it, we thank you for coming out, but we won't be inviting you back tomorrow. If your name isn't on it, we'll see you tomorrow morning at nine. We're focusing on baserunning first, so make sure you're warmed up and ready to go by then."

"I'm going to check the list," Tori said. "Why don't you finish changing and maybe figure out if you even want a girlfriend anymore, Sky."

"Tori, come on."

But Tori was already climbing off the bleachers with the other women, preparing to check to see if they'd made it to another day. Skylar waited until most of the women had climbed down. Then, she joined them in line. Tori found her on her way from checking the list and walked right past her without a word. It was Skylar's own fault; she knew that. She shook her head, wishing she could just get it together and make up her damn mind. Either she was in this thing with Tori, or she wasn't, and she needed to end it.

When she made it up to the list, there were at least ten, if not more, names on the list. They were being decisive and brutal already, and it was only day one. Thankfully, Skylar's name wasn't on it. She went to turn to go but remembered to check to see if Tori was still in the running. Not finding Tori's name, she experienced a mixed set of emotions. She was happy for Tori, but she was also a little worried that Tori being here, and their issues making themselves known daily now, would get in the way of her making a team at the end of this week.

"So, I'm going back to the dorm," Tori said when Skylar joined her at the car they had taken together that morning. "One of the girls from the team is going to drive me. Then, I'm going to shower, change, and go out to get drunk."

"Tori, you—"

"Skylar, don't. Okay?"

"I was just going to suggest you not go out and get

drunk. You made it to day two. Don't waste it by showing up hungover tomorrow."

"Fine. I'll go out for a drink or two and go back to my dorm. Tomorrow, I'll wake up early, finish packing my crap, throw it in my car, and come straight here for the try-out."

"Why are you mad at me? You wanted to try out, Tori."

"Why I'm mad at you has nothing to do with softball, Sky. Not everything has to do with softball. In fact, most things in life have nothing to do with this sport. I just wish you understood that."

Tori walked off, leaving Skylar standing there in front of her car, knowing she messed up again, but also knowing that their relationship was over. It wasn't working, and Tori wasn't going to be the one to end it, no matter how upset she was with Skylar. Skylar would have to do it herself. She lowered her head, thinking back on their two years together and wishing she would have been able to make it work.

"Everything okay, Sky?" Janine, one of the coaches Skylar had dated briefly before Tori, asked.

"Tori hates me," she replied.

"I doubt that. Seems like the opposite to me. She asked me twice today how you were doing," she said.

"She did?" Skylar asked, looking over at her.

"Yeah, she really cares about you."

"I care about her, too," Skylar replied.

"But?"

"But, what?"

"I know that tone. We dated, remember?"

"For, like, three weeks before you broke up with me because you met your future wife."

"Hey, don't make us engaged yet. We're still just girlfriends," Janine said, chuckling.

"Please, you got the ring, didn't you?"

"Last week. How'd you know?" the woman asked, smiling.

"Because I know you."

"I don't have a plan to propose yet. I just wanted to have it for that special moment in case it magically appears." Janine paused. "So, things with Tori are not headed that way?"

"I don't think so, no," Skylar replied.

"She loves you, Sky. If you're not into it, you need to tell her."

"I know. I've just been trying to get through this. I had no idea she'd gotten the call to try out until a couple of weeks ago. It's been pretty bad since."

"Do you want to grab a drink? I'm picking up the future wife, as you like to call her, and we were going to meet her sister and brother-in-law."

"No, I need to go home and ice my entire body," Skylar replied.

"Well, good luck with that." Janine started walking off. "And good luck with Tori."

CHAPTER 5

MIA had made it through the first two days of the try-out. Her shoulder was sore as hell, but she'd iced it, had taken anti-inflammatories, and was now making her way through the third day of the try-out. There had been over one hundred and fifty women the first day. Now, there were only sixty-two left, and Mia couldn't believe that she was one of them. She was one of three pitchers remaining, which made her feel like she had a fighting chance. They would probably have at least three pitchers per team. If she could just keep throwing strikes and maybe get some good hits in today, she would make it to tomorrow and, hopefully, even the final day.

"We have the cut list posted. Please take a look at it, and if your name is on it, thank you for coming out and playing with us, but we won't be inviting you back tomorrow. Make sure the office has your up-to-date contact information, though. There's always a chance we'll need people beyond the initial wave of players."

Mia did the same thing for the past two days. She sat in the bleachers and waited for the crowd around the sheet of hanging paper to dissipate. There had to be a better way than this antiquated ritual to tell players they had made the cut. Mia used the time she spent waiting to mentally prepare herself for seeing her name on that list. Then, she took a deep breath, stood, and made her way down to discover her fate.

"Hey, Mia?"

"Coach?"

"I wanted to talk to you for a second."

She had worked with Nate when she'd been on the national team. He had been a position coach back then and would be a head coach for one of the teams in the league now.

"Did they ask you to deliver the news personally or something?"

"What news?"

"That I'm cut?" she asked.

"What? Oh, no. You're not cut. Mia, you're one of the best pitchers out there. You're not getting cut."

"Really?" she asked.

"I'll admit... We didn't know what you'd bring this week. We hadn't seen you play in a while, but you've still got the stuff." He smiled and patted Mia on the shoulder. "Take it easy on that shoulder the next two days, okay? We don't want you to hurt yourself before the season starts. That's all I wanted to tell you."

"Wait. I'm on a team?"

"I don't know which one yet, but yeah, you'll be on one of them. Your hitting is still on point, and your fastball is lights-out, as always. I just noticed you seemed to be straining a bit today. Take it easy. Just go for strikes, not speed, and make sure to ice and rest."

"Yeah, I will." Mia chuckled at him. "I thought it would be a long shot to even make an alternate list."

"You've pitched better than the seven pitchers we've seen here, and from what I've heard from the other coaches around the country, you're in the top five overall. I'll be able to tell you what team at the end of the week, but don't get hurt, okay?"

"I won't. I'll take it easy."

***

Finding out that news made days four and five go a lot more smoothly for Mia, but she still worried that she wasn't good enough. That probably had more to do with her recent personal problems than her playing. She'd never doubted her talent as a softball player until her marriage began to fall apart, and she started doubting everything else. All of a sudden, she became the athlete that lacked confidence, and she hated that. It wasn't who she used to be, and she didn't want it to be the person she'd become. She focused on throwing easy strikes and on being present in all drills. When her name wasn't on the sheet for the fourth day, she let out a sigh of relief. One more day, and as long as she didn't get hurt badly, she would be on one of these teams.

She hadn't actually thought about that part. She hadn't allowed herself to think about what would happen if she made a team. She would have to move wherever she was selected. That would mean giving up her job and leaving home where her family helped support her and take care of Hazel. It would also mean moving out of state with her daughter, and she wasn't sure if Gregg would allow that or take her back to court. Technically, he'd have to approve her moving out of state in their custody agreement. Mia had never thought of reviewing that clause since she hadn't planned on moving anytime soon. She had let this whim of an idea possibly shake up her entire life. She wasn't sure she was prepared to deal with this: Gregg saying no, and her not being able to play softball like this again, or Gregg saying he didn't care, and her having to move to a new city and start over yet again.

"Hey," she said.

"What do you want, Mia? I'm busy right now."

"Gregg, can you spare five minutes to talk about your daughter?"

"Fine. Is she okay?" He sighed.

"Listen, I have the chance to play again."

"Softball? I thought you gave that up."

"I did, but there's a new league, and I have a pretty good shot of making a team."

"Okay. What does that have to do with Hazel?"

"It would mean I have to move," Mia said and then grimaced, awaiting his reply.

"Move where?"

"I don't know yet. It would depend on the team."

"So, you're asking my permission to move or something?"

"It's in the custody agreement," she reminded.

He sighed yet again and said, "Look, you and I both know I never wanted kids. We argued about it enough. I don't think I need to pretend to be something I'm not with you now."

"No, you don't."

"If you want to move – move. But I want out of child support, or at least a reduced amount."

"What? Gregg, come on. You may not have wanted kids, but you have one."

"I'm still not convinced you didn't get pregnant on purpose," he replied.

"Gregg, trust me; I did not get pregnant on purpose. We'd all but stopped having sex by then, and I wasn't planning on having your kid. It just happened. Do you honestly think that with all of our problems, I would have wanted to try to keep you by having a baby?"

"Fine. Whatever. If you want to move, just work something out so that I don't have to pay so much. I'm not getting as many hours as I thought I would when I took this damn job, so money's tight right now."

"So, you want to be less financially responsible for your daughter? Is that what I'm hearing?"

"Yeah, that's what you're hearing. If you want to move away with her, it's fine. I just need to get something out of it."

"Gregg, you don't even want to *see* her. Why are we still fighting about this?"

"Because you lied to me, Mia!" he yelled. "You lied to me when we started dating, and then even after we got married. You met some woman and–"

"And nothing happened. I didn't lie to you. We've been over this. God, part of me wishes I had never told you how I was feeling. I thought I had a husband I could trust and confide in, but your ego is so big, and it's trying to balance with your little-boy insecurities. Nothing happened with Francesca or anyone else. And just because I'm bisexual, doesn't mean I couldn't have spent the rest of my life with you. You're blaming me for something I didn't know when we met and can't control now, and you're making me – and your daughter – suffer because of it. God, just give up your parental rights, Gregg."

"You said you didn't want me to do that," he said calmly. "You said you needed the child support and that you wanted me to have a relationship with her."

"I did. And I do. But if you're going to constantly treat your daughter like an object we can barter with, I'd rather figure things out financially without you, and I'd rather you stay out of her life entirely. I don't want you popping in and out whenever it suits you or whenever you feel like you need to do something to piss me off. God, what happened to you? You weren't like this when we met."

"You weren't bisexual when we met," he argued.

"Yes, I was. I just didn't understand it back then."

"Whatever. I don't care. You're not my wife anymore. And if you want to move, work it out so that I pay nothing or at least half of what I'm paying now."

"No, I'll tell you what I'm going to do. I'm going to talk to my attorney, and you're signing the termination of parental rights paperwork. I'm not dealing with this for the next sixteen or so years."

"And why would I do that?"

"For two reasons, Gregg. Number one is that you're not this terrible person you've been pretending to be because you're hurt and angry with me. You're better than what you've become. I believe you do genuinely love your daughter. You just don't have a place for her in your life. I do. I love her more than anything, and I will provide for her.

Number two is that if you don't do this, I will tell the court about all of the women you slept with before we got separated. I'll tell my attorney to go digging. I know about that player you slept with when you were coaching high school soccer."

"She was eighteen," he replied quickly.

"I don't care how old she was. You slept with her, and you were her coach."

"It was the summer after the—"

"Gregg, stop it. Stop arguing over something you don't even want. You want to be free of all of this, don't you?"

"Yes, but—"

"Sign the papers. Let me move wherever I want to move. If you want to see your daughter in the future, and you're not fooling around with teenagers, I won't stop you. But you'll have to make an effort *if* and when that time comes."

"I'm just so angry, Mia."

"I know."

"We were supposed to be happy. We were supposed to spend our lives together. I was going to play pro ball until I retired. You were going to win gold medals. We weren't going to have kids. We were going to travel and just enjoy our lives. What happened?"

"There's a long answer to that question. Do you really want it?" she asked back.

"Can you give me the short version?"

"You stopped trying, Gregg," Mia offered. "You got used to being number one in school. And when you had to work harder and harder just to make the team, you didn't like that, so you stopped trying. You stopped trying at soccer. You stopped trying with us. Then, you cheated. You used me discovering something about myself as a reason why the world was against you, and pushed me away and away until you decided you couldn't live with it anymore." She paused and leaned back against the pillow. "You didn't want to talk about what I was feeling or ask me if I was still committed to our marriage, which I was at the time. You just wanted it to be over. We had one night of make-up sex that I thought would be us just saying goodbye to that part of our relationship, and–"

"You got pregnant."

"And you wanted me to terminate," she added. "I couldn't do that. I wanted her, Gregg. I want her. If nothing else came out of our marriage, and I had to deal with all of this shit, at least I got her. I wouldn't change that for anything."

"What are you going to do?" he asked.

"I guess we'll see what city they want me to move to. If it works, I'll do it. The pay isn't going to be good. I'm going to have to get a job wherever I go, and there's childcare to figure out since my mom is at home, but… I'll be okay."

"I'll do what you're asking, okay? I'll sign the termination papers."

"Really?" she asked, leaning back up again.

"It's just easier this way. I'll try to send you money when I can, though, okay? It won't be regular or anything, but when I have some, I'll send it."

"That would help."

"And if I can get my brain sorted around all of this stuff, maybe I'll ask to see her someday."

"We can talk about that then, okay?" Mia asked, not wanting to commit to that just yet.

"I'll call my lawyer tomorrow. I'm sure he'd love to get another hour or two out of me so he can add that money to his boat fund."

"Gregg?"

"Yeah?"

"This is for the best," she said.

"I guess. I used to think you and I being together was for the best."

"It's not now, though," she replied.

"No, it's not," he agreed. "Just make sure I have your address, okay?"

"I will once I have one," she said.

"Fine. I'll let you go then. I have to get back."

Mia knew he didn't have anything to get back to. He had always liked to appear busy, even when he wasn't.

"Thank you for doing this."

"Yeah," he said and hung up the phone.

CHAPTER 6

"YOU made it," Skylar said when she saw Tori's name on the sheet.

It was the end of the final day of try-outs, and today's list – the final list, had the names of the players that *had* made one of the eight teams. Tori's name was on it, and surprisingly to Skylar, so was her own.

"You did, too. Congratulations, Sky," Tori said, placing a hand on the small of Skylar's back. "You're staying here."

"Looks like it," Skylar said.

"And I'm going to Boise," Tori replied. "Boise... I never thought I'd end up in Boise."

"So, you're going?"

"I made it this far. I might as well see it through at least for the exhibition season, right?"

"I guess so," Skylar said; her happiness dampened due to what she was about to talk to Tori about. "Hey, we should talk."

"It's fine, Sky." Tori walked next to her toward the parking lot.

"What's fine?" Sky asked, turning toward her.

"We're over. I get it," Tori said.

"Wait. We should talk, Tor. Come back to my place, and–"

"Now you *want* me at your place? You've been avoiding me for weeks. I don't think we've kissed for days, let alone had sex. You don't want this anymore."

"Tor, I'm sorry. I've just got a lot–"

"If you say you have a lot going on, I'm going to punch your shoulder." Tori lifted an eyebrow. "We all have a lot going on, Sky. Either you want to be in a relationship with me, or you don't. If you do, you make it work. If you don't, you have the courage to tell me." She paused on a sigh. "You tell me I'm immature sometimes, but you're just as bad, if not worse. At least I can say the words out loud. It's not working. I love you, and you don't love me anymore."

"I care about you, Tor."

"I don't just want someone to care about me. I want someone to love me; to be madly *in love* with me. I want someone who wants me how I want them."

"I know."

"I want that for you, too, Sky." Tori bounced her head back and forth as if considering something. "Well, not right now. Right now, the thought of you being with anyone else makes me want to get violent with you, and then… And then, to puke after. But I want you to be happy. It's just not with me, is it?"

"I don't think so," Skylar replied.

"I'm going to Boise anyway. So, the timing is right, I think. I have some stuff at your place. Can I come by and pick it up?"

"Anytime you want," Skylar said.

"You're lucky. You get to stay here."

"Yeah, I guess."

"I'll swing by tomorrow and get everything. Then, I guess I'll see you next at the first game we play against each other."

"It's weird that it's just ending like this. I mean, it was two years, Tor."

"It was a good two years, but I'd rather get home so I can cry into my pillow instead of crying in front of my future teammates and competition."

"Tor…"

"You were going to be my one, Sky. I know you think I'm young, and that I'm being an idealist or something, but I loved you. I still love you. So I need to get out of here and take care of that whole crying thing, like, now, okay?"

Skylar watched her now ex-girlfriend walk away. When she got home, she couldn't celebrate making the team. She could only think about how she'd hurt Tori. There was a time where she thought they'd end up together, too. She wished that were still the case, but at the same time, it probably wouldn't work now that they were going to be living in two different states and playing against each other in at least a few games in this shortened season.

Skylar showered first. Then, she tried to make things easier on Tori by packing up what she could find and setting it in a box by the door. She stared at the box, realizing it might be harsh for Tori to see that right when she walked in – like Skylar couldn't wait to get rid of her stuff, so she shoved it back into her bedroom. Then, she laid down to review the contract that had been emailed to her earlier that evening. The money she'd make wasn't nearly enough to support herself. She would have to get a part-time job coaching somewhere, and she couldn't do that at the national team level. There were a few high schools nearby and many colleges. She might be able to get something at one of them, but she would need to find something soon. Once the other players reviewed their contracts, and many of them moved to town, the jobs related to their sport, that were actually available, would dry up, because they were all in the same women-playing-pro-sports-that-didn't-pay-nearly-enough boat.

Skylar searched for job openings on a couple of job boards she knew about, and applied for one that wouldn't pay much but would supplement her income. Then, she went on the regular sites and found a few hourly jobs that would do in case that one didn't pan out. She'd work customer service jobs if she had to. She just wanted to play ball. After she reviewed what was out there and applied for a couple of things, Skylar decided to do some research on her new teammates. She had taken a picture of the list for the Oklahoma City Boomers and looked up the players she didn't already know.

She was lucky. There were three national team members on this squad that she'd worked with. There was someone else that she'd heard of but had left the team before Skylar had arrived as a coach. Skylar had known *of* her as the woman had been coming up, but only by name. Mia Landis was, according to everyone, an amazing pitcher. She had been six years ahead of Skylar, so they hadn't run across one another in the softball circles. From what Skylar had heard, she'd retired early, but not due to injury. Skylar typed her name into the browser and clicked on the top result.

"Fuck," she whispered to herself.

Mia Landis was beautiful. She had bright-green eyes and blonde hair that was pulled back through her hat in this picture. Skylar scrolled down and found a few more pictures. One was of Mia pitching. Another one had been taken of her standing at the plate with the bat in her seemingly confident hands. Skylar scrolled back up to learn more about the woman who would be pitching for her team and liked the stats she saw on the page. She wondered why the woman had left the team. Her numbers were great, and she hadn't gotten injured. She'd been an all-around star in high school, college, and at the national level. Why would she give that up if she didn't have to? Why would anyone?

***

"I can't believe you're leaving us," Megan said.

"I know. But you know I planned to play again when I could."

Skylar sat in the office of her boss, Megan Kitchens, the current head coach of the national team, delivering her resignation in person as well as in the email she'd sent that morning.

"You're a pitcher, Sky. Are you sure you want to switch to catching?"

"I'm sure I want to play. Doc says I'll never pitch again unless there's a miracle or something. If I do, I'll never be as good as I was before."

"I'm sorry to hear that."

"If I have any chance of making Paris, I need to join this league and switch positions. Catcher makes the most sense, and the coaches noticed something in me, or they wouldn't have given me the shot in the league."

"Are you planning on joining us as a player in Paris?" she asked with a smile.

"That's the plan."

"You know we've got the two best catchers in the world on our roster right now, right?"

"I do. But one of them is thirty-three and not likely to keep playing for the next three years, and the other one is twenty-eight and got married last year. I seem to recall her mentioning that she had the dream of making an Olympic team – which she did for Tokyo – and then having a few kids."

"You're using your insider knowledge of this team for evil, Sky." Megan laughed.

"I'm just planning ahead. I thought about outfield, but that's another skill set entirely, and I've never played there before."

"Plus, we have young outfielders who aren't likely to retire or pop out kids anytime soon," Megan said.

"Exactly. First base and short are good to go. I tried second base in little league, and I wasn't a fan. Third base is fine, but I had experience catching."

"This isn't a job interview for Paris. You know that, right?"

"I do." Skylar laughed. "But I am glad I get to stay here."

"Me too, Sky. Look… I can't have you on full-time staff if you're playing in the league, but I can keep you on part-time as a scout."

"Wait. Really?"

"We're not officially affiliated with the league. *You* will be once you sign that contract. You'll be up close and personal with some of the athletes, but we'd expect you to do a little more than that, obviously."

"Yeah, okay. That would be great, actually."

"Can you work out the details with the office?"

"Sure."

"And you know we can't pay much, right? If you find us some gems out there that we don't already know about, we'll be able to do more for you if they actually make the team."

"It's fine. Anything helps."

"Great. Then, I'm deleting this resignation letter. Go down the hall and chat with Nancy. She'll work through the rest of the details with you. You'll be expected to join the weekly meetings anytime you're not on the road."

"Not a problem. Thanks, Megan. I was about to work from home doing Amazon customer support," she replied as she stood.

"Well, don't do that unless you have to. I know the sacrifices our players have to make just to play this sport."

"Thanks, Megan. Really. I mean it. I'd love to do this and stay on board here. It's not just about me making the Paris team. It's about me being a part of this. Even if I don't get to be a part of it as a player, I'd still like to be there on staff."

"Let's forget about this whole resignation thing then." Megan winked at her. "Hey, I heard Mia Landis is on your team."

"She is, yeah. Why?'

"She was on Team USA for a while. Then, she left. I thought she was done playing, but she's an amazing pitcher. She's once in a generation good. If she's back playing, I'd like you to check her out for us."

"Really?"

"Yeah. If she's as good as she was just a few years ago, she's a definite contender for the squad."

"Okay. I'll check her out," Skylar replied.

"It's a shame you two missed each other. She left not long before you got here."

"Can I ask why?"

"She didn't give a specific reason at first, but she has a daughter now, so I can guess that was probably the reason. It's interesting, though. When she left, she told us she was done playing for good. I didn't expect her to come back."

"Plenty of women come back to sports after they have babies, Megan."

"I'm well aware, Sky. I'm just saying she didn't seem like *she* would."

"Well, I guess I'll find out soon enough. She's one of three pitchers, and I'm one of two catchers, so we'll be working pretty closely together."

CHAPTER 7

"HE signed the papers?" Mia's mother asked.

"He did. He was actually kind of okay about it, surprisingly. Maybe he's near the end of processing his anger, or maybe he just realized finally that this would get him off the hook as a father."

"So, that's it?" the woman asked.

"He said he'll send money occasionally. When I saw him to sign the papers, he handed me two hundred bucks and said that was the best he could do right now."

"That's better than nothing. I still can't believe he gave in after all that fighting he put you through."

"I think he finally just gave up. It's hard to be angry for that long, and he's been angry for a long time."

"I guess so. Well, I'm glad it's over. I'm sad it means you can move, though." Her mother hugged her. "But I know how important this is to you."

"It's a long drive, Mom. We have to get going. It's going to take me three days just to get there, with Hazel and having to stop to sleep."

"I know. I'm just going to miss you both so much. I'd wake her up to hug and kiss her, but if she's out now, that's a good thing for you."

"Mom, I love you. Thank you so much for everything."

"I love you, baby. Drive safe. Call me along the way, and when you get there. I'll try to make it to the first game I can, okay?"

"I know. I love you," Mia repeated and kissed her mother's cheek.

She hopped into the car, looking out the window at her waving mother and then back at her sleeping child, put the car in reverse, and headed down the driveway toward

51

the interstate; the first of many that she'd take over the next three days to get her to her new one-bedroom apartment in Oklahoma City, Oklahoma. She never thought she'd be living in Oklahoma, but it was as good a place as any to get a new start, away from Gregg, and back to the sport she used to love more than anything in the world until she had that baby in the backseat.

***

Mia was exhausted. She'd just driven her two-year-old across the country, pulling all of their worldly possessions behind them in the moving container hitched to her car. They'd slept in cheap hotels along the way, and she wanted nothing more than to get them settled into their new apartment. That meant moving in everything herself while keeping Hazel busy with toys. She had brought her own bed and planned to buy a toddler bed for Hazel in town. After several hours of moving in their stuff and placing the mattress on the floor because she had no energy left over to put the bed together, she made the bed with sheets and a blanket and got Hazel settled into it with pillows lining the sides. Then, she made herself a quick meal of soup and showered before she joined her daughter. She had her first day of team meetings tomorrow, and she needed to get at least a little rest.

When she woke up the following morning to her daughter politely smacking her stomach, claiming she was hungry, Mia pulled Hazel in for a nice, long hug. She kissed her cheek and got out of bed. She made breakfast for them both, dressed Hazel, and then got the little girl busy again with her toys before she readied herself for work. She packed up their things and dropped Hazel off at the daycare she had researched endlessly online, paying them in advance for the full week since that was cheaper, and hoping she could find something cheaper still, but with a reputable place or person. It would be tough until she found something else to supplement her team income. She had a lead on a coaching gig, but it would be tricky to do both coaching and playing since they would be in season at the same time. She would have to be an assistant or position coach, and the team would have to be okay with her being gone some of the time.

When Mia made it to the field, she sat in her car for a few minutes, feeling those nerves she used to get before a big game returning to her. She inhaled deeply and drank some water from her bottle. Then, she gathered herself and climbed out of the car, not really well-rested or ready for her first day on a new team. But it was supposed to be meetings more than anything today, so, hopefully, she could sleep better tonight and be ready to go tomorrow.

"Mia, hey," Lara Hector greeted.

"Hey, Lara. We're on the same team again," Mia replied, hugging her old teammate.

"College wasn't it for us, I guess. How have you been? I heard you were out of the game."

"I was for a while. I've been coaching since I got pregnant. My team had just won state, actually. I got a chance to be there right before I moved here."

"That's awesome. So, you've been wanting to get back? I heard you were done."

"I thought I was." They started walking. "I was going to keep coaching, but one of the players on the team heard about the league, and I thought I was just crazy enough to give it a try."

"Crazy enough? I think you mean talented enough. You always were the best pitcher, girl. You know that." Lara bumped shoulders with Mia. "Hey, Skylar!"

A woman Mia didn't know had been walking in front of them, carrying her bat bag over her shoulder. The woman turned around, and Mia stopped walking for a second. Skylar smiled in Lara's direction, and Lara walked ahead of Mia to hug her. Mia stood back and watched as the two women talked. Skylar had light-brown hair about shoulder-length, but as she spoke with Lara, she pulled it back, revealing a long neck and skin that was tan, leading Mia to believe she spent a lot of time outside. That was when she remembered. She had seen this woman before. The camera was usually on the field during the Olympics, but every so often, it would pan to the dugout, and Mia remembered seeing this woman there next to Team USA's head coach. She was a member of the coaching staff. What was she doing here, dressed like she was ready to play? Maybe she was an assistant and just always dressed like a player. Mia didn't know, but she walked up to the two women because regardless of her position, Mia would need to get to know her sooner or later.

"Hi," Skylar said when she saw Mia approaching. "Mia, right?"

"Yeah. How'd you—"

"I was a pitching coach on the national team," Skylar replied.

"Oh, well, it's nice to meet you." Mia held out her hand.

"Skylar. Sorry, I should have said that first. Skylar Donahue," the woman said, holding out her own hand for Mia to shake.

"Are you the pitching coach?" Mia asked her as she shook it, feeling the strong shake in just about every part of her.

"No, I'm playing, actually." Skylar nodded. "Lara and I know each other because she was on the national team in Tokyo."

"You're playing?" Mia asked.

"Yeah, catcher."

"I thought you were a pitching coach," Mia said.

"Sky was a pitcher. She got hurt, though. That's why she wasn't on the national team. She probably would have been otherwise, but she's been rehabbing it and made the team as a catcher."

"You're okay now, though," Mia said more than asked.

"Yeah, it's still healing, but I'm not going through the same arm motions that were causing the problems before, so that's good. You're a pitcher, though. So, we'll probably be spending some time together." The woman gave her what Mia guessed was a forced smile.

"I guess so." She gave a smile back.

"We're going to be late if you keep chatting out here, so let's go inside. I'm sure they're going to make us do trust falls or some bullshit like that just to get to know each other," Lara said.

The three women walked through the gate that led to the dugout. They hung their bat bags on the chain-link fence and made their way to the bleachers, where they saw other players hanging out. They joined them, with Lara sitting on the other side of Skylar, leaving Mia sitting next to the woman she was pretty sure she had just been checking out a minute ago. She hadn't checked out a woman in a while, and she was still a rookie at this whole being-attracted-to-women thing. She also wasn't about to start anything with a new teammate. If she'd met Skylar at a bar, though, and Skylar was into women, she'd definitely be someone Mia would want to talk to and maybe even do a little more with.

"You okay?"

"Huh?" Mia asked her.

"I asked if you were okay. They just gave a whole speech about the game plan, and you seemed a little out of it."

"What? Who did? They did?" Mia looked around at the coaches who were standing off to the side of first base.

"I'm kidding," Skylar said, smiling at her. "You just looked really serious there for a second."

"Oh, sorry."

"You don't have to apologize," Skylar replied. "It's a little overwhelming, isn't it?"

"Yeah, I never thought I'd be playing again, so I think this is going to be an adjustment."

"Why?"

"Why the adjustment?" Mia asked.

"No, why didn't you think you'd ever play again?" Skylar asked back.

"Oh, I—"

"All right, let's get started," one of the coaches Mia didn't recognize began. "Today is a meet-and-greet, followed by a light warm-up and fitness test. We need to know what we're starting with. Tomorrow is when the fun begins." The woman laughed. "We'll start this morning just by going around and introducing ourselves. The coaches will start, and then we'll go through all the players. My name is Cheryl Mastriani. Before taking this job, I was a head coach at Nebraska. I played second base for Washington State before that. I've been coaching now for about ten years, and when they asked me to head up one of these teams, I couldn't wait to sign up. I would have killed for a league like this as a player, and I'm excited to get to coach you all as we try to make a legit pro softball league happen in the US after many other failed attempts. If there ever was a time for this, it was now."

There were some cheers from the group. Skylar actually clapped and gave a cheer. Mia yawned because she was exhausted, not because she didn't like the speech.

"Not a fan of the message?" Skylar asked her.

"What? No, I am. Sorry. Was it that noticeable?"

"No, I was just looking at you."

Mia turned to her, surprised. Skylar looked away at the same time. Mia shook her head and turned back to the coaching staff.

"Let's go around and get to know everyone," Cheryl said.

The two other coaches introduced themselves and gave a bit about their coaching and playing histories. Then, they opened it up to the players.

"My name is Gaby. I just graduated from San Diego State. I play first base," one young woman said.

"I'm Tasha. I play third, and I've been playing on the

56

national team since I graduated from BU," she said of Boston University.

"My name is Leslie Potter, but I go by Potter. I'm a shortstop. I played for Michigan," she said.

"Stephanie. Outfield. Typically, right field. Florida State. I had one year left, but I didn't want to miss the first season of the new league, so I tried out, and here I am," she said.

The introductions continued. Mia listened to all of them, including Lara's. None of these women was actually over the age of twenty-five. Most were twenty-two and fresh graduates from their school's softball program. Mia hadn't played in over two years, with the exception of throwing the ball around a little and taking some swings at the local batting cages. She had practiced with her team, but she was a coach. She didn't actually play. She mainly just helped with warm-ups and drills. These women were all in shape and ready to go out and play.

"I'm Skylar." She waved, and Mia turned to her. "I pitched for UCLA. I've been a pitching coach for the national team since graduating a few years ago, but I'm ready to play again. I'll be catching for the team, though."

Mia did the math. If she graduated a few years ago, that would make her twenty-five or maybe twenty-four. She could also be twenty-six. Mia wasn't great with ages. She tried to think about something else, but Skylar elbowed her and then nodded.

"Oh, me. I'm Mia. I'm a pitcher. I was on the national team for a bit after school. I've been coaching locally since I left the team, and now I'm ready to get back out there."

Was that a good introduction? She didn't know. A few more women introduced themselves. Then, the coach took over.

"We know that this isn't a full-time job for most of you; maybe even all of you. We'll be meeting with all of you individually to talk about what the schedule will look like because we realize a start-up league like this isn't going to pay enough to support you or your families. We want to make sure we have an understanding of what you each need, and if there's anything we can help you with, we'll do what we can. I have a list of local jobs related to softball, baseball, and other sports if any of you are interested in hearing about them. We're also planning a team-building event this weekend. Coach Tom, here, is a local." Cheryl hooked a thumb toward the assistant coach to her right. "He's offered up his house Friday night for a welcome backyard barbecue. Then, we'll leave from there and go to Lake Thunderbird State Park. We'll be carpooling, so make friends this week and decide who's riding with whom. We'll leave early evening to get there in time to set up camp. We've got tents ready for you all. We'll come back Sunday afternoon, so make your plans. Welcome to the Boomers, ladies," Cheryl said.

CHAPTER 8

"HEY, do you have weekend options?" Skylar heard Mia ask into her phone as they took a break from practice to grab some water. "No? What if I pay extra?" There was a pause. "Okay. No. Yeah. I'll have to find somewhere else. Do you have a place you recommend for the days you're full or–" She paused again. "Okay. Thank you. Yeah, I'll be there as soon as I'm done here. Thanks." Mia hung up the phone and turned back around suddenly.

"Sorry. I wasn't trying to snoop. Coach asked me to tell you that we're back from the water break." Skylar pointed at the women heading to the field.

"Oh, thanks." Mia locked her phone and looked down at the ground. "Actually, do you think you can give me one more minute?"

"Sure. I'm just the messenger," Skylar said, backing up. "But they want pitchers and catchers working out together, so you might want to hurry."

"I will. Thanks," Mia said again.

Skylar walked backward for a bit before she turned around and headed through the dugout to the field. She was already wearing her gear, save her mask, but she grabbed her glove off the bench and made her way to the small patches of dirt that would act as their bullpen at this borrowed practice field.

"You're working with Mia today, Sky," Tom told her. "We're going to have you two start off together, see how it goes, and if it's not working, we'll put you with Jenny," he said, speaking of one of the other pitchers on the team.

"Okay," she replied.

"Where is Mia?" he asked, looking around the field.

"She needed another minute," Skylar said it and hated having to say it.

She took her job very seriously. She didn't like someone else treating it like it wasn't important. It was one of the reasons she and Tori had ended. There were other reasons, of course, but Tori saw this league as something she could do right now until something better came along. Skylar saw this league *as* the something better and didn't want to think about not playing again.

"Jenny's warmed up. Do you want to start with her today? We can have Mia work out with–"

"Sorry. I'm here." Mia rushed over to them, breathing hard. "Just had to take care of something real quick. Sorry."

"We start back from our breaks on time, Mia," Tom told her, and Skylar looked away.

"I know. I apologize. I–"

"Just work with Skylar. She's a former pitcher, so you two should be good together. Let's get the knee drill going. Sky, can you catch for her? We don't have a wall out here. You're a coach. Watch her form." He walked off without waiting for a response.

"You ready?" Skylar asked.

"What just happened?" Mia asked her.

"Knee drill. You know that one, right?"

"Of course, I know that one. I've been pitching my whole life."

"Then, what's the problem?"

"You're a catcher, and he just asked you to coach me. Then, he left."

"I *am* a pitching coach for the national team. Well, I was until I came here," she replied. "And, like he said, I *was* a pitcher."

Mia looked off, and Skylar watched her sigh.

"I guess I'll just do the knee drill then, to get warmed up," she said.

"Sounds good to me," Skylar replied, sliding her mask over her face, despite not really needing it.

She then moved back into her spot and turned around, waiting for Mia to get into position. Mia got on her knees and started in the open-door position with a cocked wrist. Then, she swung back without a ball just to get the motion down, doing a full windmill, and pretended to throw the ball toward Skylar. She picked up a ball off the ground. Skylar held out her glove. Then, Mia threw the ball her way for real.

The first few pitches were just warm-ups. Skylar watched Mia's perfect form. Her back was straight. She didn't bend or move improperly. She used her shoulder to propel the ball forward and her wrist to snap it in the right direction and follow through. By the second set of fifteen pitches, though, Skylar had to admit, she was more than impressed. Mia definitely had speed, and she wasn't even trying. Every one of her tosses had been right into Skylar's glove. That wasn't crazy difficult. Skylar was only about twenty feet away. She was still pretty impressed, though. After the final set, Mia stood up.

"I'm ready for something a little harder," she said.

"Pitch it for real then." Skylar stood and moved back behind the plate to kneel in the proper position.

"Are you sure?" Mia asked.

"Give me what you've got, pitch," she encouraged, smacking the inside of her glove with her fist.

Mia stood with her hand inside her glove, likely moving the ball into just the position she wanted to get the proper grip. Skylar held out her glove, not knowing what pitch Mia was about to throw. Mia wound up and let the ball fly. Before Skylar knew it, the ball hit her glove.

"Fuck," she said softly to herself.

That hurt. She removed the ball from her glove and tossed it back to Mia. Mia threw hard. If Skylar had to guess, Mia threw harder than she had, and she'd been known for her speed.

"Again?"

"Let's go for it," Skylar said.

Skylar braced herself for the next pitch, expecting it to be slower or maybe an off-speed, but Mia gave her another fastball. She resisted the urge to wince as the ball smacked into the thoroughly padded glove. Skylar tossed it back.

"Change-up?"

"Yeah," Skylar replied.

Mia gave her a couple of off-speed pitches. They were perfect.

"Now what?"

"What else you got?" Skylar asked.

"Just about everything," Mia said. "I've got two fastballs, a change-up, a curve, knuckle, and a screw."

"Screw, huh?" Skylar teased.

"Yeah, I've got a screw–" Mia stopped herself. "Oh, I see what you did there."

Mia pitched. Skylar caught. Then, the team got together for the end of the day meeting. Skylar sat down next to Jenny, whom she'd known from her playing days, and took a long drink of water. Being in that gear for hours on end was uncomfortable and hot, but other than that, she found herself enjoying catching. She wasn't as experienced as their other catcher, Kai, who had been catching since she'd popped out of her mother's womb, but she thought she could give her a run for her money if she had better chemistry with their two main pitchers. Jenny and Mia were both up for the starting job opening day. Skylar wanted to make sure *she* was, too.

"She's amazing, isn't she?" Jenny asked as everyone continued to settle.

"Who?"

"Mia. I was watching her workout before. She's just as good as I heard."

"You're pretty good, too, there, Jen. There's a reason you're here," Skylar replied.

"Yeah, but I'm much better as a reliever. Plus, she's got every pitch in the book. I've got a good curveball and a decent change-up, but that's it outside of my fastball."

"That's enough," Skylar said.

"They gave me Kai to work with." Jenny bumped

shoulders with Skylar. "I think that bodes well for you."

"What do you mean?"

"Just that Mia is the obvious starter. If you're working with her, that probably means you two are the A-team all the way."

"It's the first week. We don't know what's happening yet," she said.

"I'd heard she was done. No one knew she'd planned on playing again."

"Mia?"

"Yeah, she was a huge loss to the US. You'd know that."

"I never met her before this week. I only knew *of* her."

"And you're telling me that no one ever told you how good she was before?"

"No, they did, but it didn't matter to me. I had the pitchers I had. Mia Landis wasn't playing anymore, so it didn't make sense to focus on a pitcher I wasn't coaching."

"Well, I think you should focus on her now."

Skylar glanced over at Mia, noting her blonde hair that was braided today though still pulled back into her ever-present hat. The woman was sitting off to the side of the group now. She seemed deep in thought again. She always seemed deep in thought, though, unless she was pitching. When Mia pitched, it appeared to Skylar that Mia was only focused on the ball hitting the target and nothing else.

"I'll go talk to her for a second," Skylar said and moved to stand.

"Okay. Tomorrow night is the big barbeque. Tom has meat for the meat lovers, veggie burgers for the vegetarians, and I'm bringing the side dishes," Cheryl said as she moved in front of where they were all sitting. "Make sure you're packed and ready to go. We have the carpool list and will email everyone after practice. Be at Tom's no later than noon. We're not drinking tomorrow since we'll be driving, and we're in training, so be prepared to make small talk while sober." Cheryl laughed at her own joke, which made the rest of them remain silent. "Get some rest tonight. Ice those arms and knees. Mia and Skylar, can I see you before you head out?"

The rest of the team stood and began making their way toward the parking lot as one collective group. Skylar remained sitting and looked over at Mia, who appeared to be just as concerned as Skylar. Cheryl moved to sit down next to Skylar on the bleachers. Mia took the hint and moved closer to the two women, dropping her bat bag onto the step below them.

"Hey, ladies. How are you liking things so far?"

"It's been great playing again," Skylar replied.

"Yeah," Mia agreed but didn't offer anything else.

"We know both of you are just getting back into things physically, and we don't want you to wear yourselves out, so make sure you follow the physio's instructions when they tell you to rest, ice, heat, medicate, and even pray, okay?"

Mia laughed. Skylar looked over at her and worked to hide her smile.

"Understood," Skylar said, returning her attention to her coach.

"Listen, it's no secret that Mia, here, would have been in Tokyo as the starting pitcher had she not retired early. You're one of the best we've ever seen."

"But?" Mia guessed.

"But?" Cheryl tossed back.

"But, I'm number two, or just too old, or–"

"No, Mia." Cheryl chuckled. "You're still just as good as you used to be. Your arm is a rocket that never needs to refuel, apparently. I was just going to say that I'd like you and Skylar to remain working together. I'm pairing Kai with Jenny for now. She'll be our reliever and start when you need a break. This season is a short one, but we're taking fitness seriously. Skylar is coming off an injury she likes to pretend she doesn't have." She gave Skylar an accusing eyebrow. "You two know how important chemistry is between a pitcher and a catcher. Tom and I were talking.

We think Kai and Jenny will work well enough together, but, Skylar, you and Jenny know one another and get along already. If you and Mia can work well together, too, that makes you the starting catcher by default."

"That's amazing. Thanks, Cheryl," Skylar said, trying again to hide her smile.

"Don't thank me yet. You need to see the physio about that wrist. You have to be able to snap it when you follow through on those throws to second base, Sky. Make sure it's in good shape, okay?"

"Yes, ma'am," she said.

"Mia, Skylar's driving tomorrow. You're heading out there with her. Any objections?"

"Oh, no. That's fine."

"Great. Use the drive and this weekend to get to know one another better, okay?"

Mia and Skylar both nodded as Cheryl stood and left them alone.

"So, I guess we have to get to know each other, huh?" Skylar asked, turning to face Mia.

"I guess so," Mia replied.

CHAPTER 9

MIA had the morning off, which meant she could get in a light workout in her living room before Hazel woke up. One of the unique things about her daughter was that she didn't wake up at five in the morning like a lot of toddlers. She usually slept right up until Mia woke her. As Hazel lay in the small bed Mia had bought the afternoon prior and had put together the night before, Mia turned on the TV in the living room. She put the volume on mute and worked out along with the instructor. After about thirty minutes, she made her way to the bathroom to shower. She checked on Hazel when she got out to find her still asleep. She couldn't resist walking over and running her hand through the girl's hair. As she did, she felt her daughter's forehead and noticed that Hazel was warmer than she ought to be.

Mia had been through this enough times by now not to freak out, so she made her way back to the bathroom to rifle through the supplies she'd brought with her. She grabbed the thermometer and went back to her daughter, placing it in her ear and checking the read-out all while the little girl slept. It was ninety-nine; not the highest temperature she'd had but also not normal for Hazel, who regularly ran right around ninety-eight point six. Mia went to the kitchen to make them both breakfast and grabbed the fever medicine to try to convince her sometimes obstinate child to take it. She could not be sick.

Mia was due at the barbeque later, and then, she was gone for the weekend. She'd managed to find a babysitter to watch Mia all weekend, which was a miracle and a costly one at that. She had used what was left over from her small relocation allowance to pay for the woman she'd chatted with on the phone, met in person after practice the previous night, and then read through all the online reviews just to make sure she wasn't leaving her child with the wrong person.

She had not been prepared to have to leave her with someone overnight so soon. She had wanted to work out the network of daycares and babysitters in the area before the first away game, make sure she took the time to pick the right one, and figure out a routine or a schedule for when she had to be away. This whole weekend thing was throwing a major wrench in her plan.

Hazel woke slowly, as she usually did. Mia gave her time to adjust to being awake before she called her to the table. Hazel did that adorable walk that was more waddle than an actual walk. Mia helped her into her chair, and they ate breakfast together. Mia argued with her child, but Hazel gave into the medicine seeing no other way out.

As Hazel played on the floor of the living room, Mia readied herself for the barbeque. She threw on a pair of well-worn jeans and a t-shirt, choosing to go casual for the day. She had no idea what to pack to go camping, but the coaching staff had explained that they would bring all the essentials. The players only had to bring what they needed to be away for the weekend, so she tossed a few things into her duffle bag. The doorbell rang just as she placed her hand on Hazel's head to check her temperature again.

"Hi," Mia greeted the older woman who would be taking care of her child.

"Hello again," the woman replied with a warm smile. "There she is," she said to Hazel just as warmly, if not more so.

"I appreciate you picking her up. I'd let you stay here,

but we're still moving in."

"It's not a problem at all. I just dropped my oldest son off at his summer camp, so I was on my way home anyway. And my house is a daycare Monday through Friday. It's already set up for little miss Hazel," the woman explained.

"I packed her things already. I had to throw some fever medicine in there, though. I think she's okay, but she was a little hot this morning," Mia told her. "Maybe I shouldn't go."

"You have to go somewhere for work, right?"

"Yeah, it's a team-building thing for my new job. I can't really miss it, but… I don't know. If she's got a fever, I should stay."

The woman knelt in front of Hazel and placed a hand gently on the occupied girl's forehead.

"She'll be fine. She's hardly hot now. I'll make sure she takes medicine again, and I'll check her temperature every few hours. I'll call you immediately if her fever worsens. And, you said you were camping when we talked?"

"Yes, but I've been told the cell reception should be fine."

"Thunderbird?"

"Yeah. Have you been?"

"Many times. You'll be fine. I'll take good care of her, I promise. I'm a mother of three myself. I know how hard this is for you right now, but she's in good hands," the woman said, smiling up at Mia.

***

An hour later, Mia was standing outside her apartment building. Since she was carpooling with Skylar, Skylar was picking her up, and they'd go to Tom's place together and then straight to the state park. Hazel had cried when she'd been placed in the car seat in her new babysitter's car. It had just about killed Mia. She hadn't spent even a night away from Mia since the girl had been born up until recently, when she had to travel for the try-out. She had been gone for hours at a time before that, but not for one full night. Gregg hadn't exactly been reliable, so she had never felt like she had a choice.

When a modest but new-looking car pulled up in front of her, and the window rolled down, Mia leaned down to get a look.

"Are you ready?" Skylar asked.

"Yeah."

"You can toss your stuff in the trunk," she replied.

Mia walked to the back of the car and tossed her bag in, closing the trunk and climbing into Skylar's car.

"Thanks for driving," she said.

"No problem. They asked for volunteers the other day, and I prefer to be behind the wheel whenever possible."

"Yeah? I think that says something about you, doesn't it?" Mia tried to joke.

"That a friend of mine was driving one night when I was in the passenger's seat, and she almost got us killed? Yeah." Skylar put the car in drive and pulled out of the parking lot.

"Oh, I'm sorry. I was honestly just joking. I–"

"So was I," Skylar interrupted and chuckled. "It says I'm a bit of a control freak, I guess. It's probably why I loved pitching so much."

"And why you moved behind the plate after your injury?" Mia asked.

"It's the next best thing, in my opinion. In one way or another, I'm involved in every play."

Mia's phone chimed with a notification. She looked down to see the note from her sitter that Hazel was doing just fine. She was playing, and her temperature seemed normal.

"Right," Mia replied, not fully taking in what Skylar had just said.

"You okay?"

"Yeah. Why?"

"I don't know. You just seemed distracted," Skylar said.

"No, I'm good," she denied.

"Tom lives, like, five minutes from here. So, we'll be on time if that's what you're worried about. Sorry, I was a little late. I needed to stop for gas."

"I'm not worried," Mia replied. Then, she shook her head. "Sorry, I'm not worried or upset that you were late. It was, like, five minutes, and I was running behind anyway, so it worked out."

"Okay," Skylar replied, seeming to brush it off more than actually think it was okay.

"So, how's the wrist?" Mia decided to try small talk.

"Fine. Why?"

"I don't know. I guess I was just trying to start a conversation."

"And you start with an old injury? Is that how they make conversation where you're from?"

"How do they make conversation where *you're* from?"

"Not with the heavy stuff." Skylar laughed. "I think we pick a nice, safe topic like where you grew up first, and then move into the deeper stuff if we want to later."

"Okay. Well, I grew up in Columbus, Ohio. But we moved to just outside of Pittsburgh right before high school. It's a smallish town, but with a big city nearby."

"You went to Florida, right?" Skylar asked as she turned the car.

"Yeah."

"UCLA," Skylar said of herself.

"I remember from intro day," Mia said.

"Right," Skylar replied. Then, she turned to Mia as they sat at a stoplight. "So, what was Columbus like?"

"Boring. Where did you grow up?"

"Middle of nowhere," Skylar said.

"That's specific," Mia replied.

"Bible belt. You wouldn't know the name of my tiny town anyway. Let's just say I never really fit in. I love my family, but I don't really like them all that much, and I'm here because the national team is here and now this team, so there's that, I guess."

"Got it," Mia said. "Siblings?"

"Two brothers. You?"

"None," she replied. "Only child."

"Must be nice. Brothers suck." Skylar turned the car down a residential street. "I don't know if sisters are the same, but brothers are a pain in the ass."

"Did they pick on you or something?"

"Or something," Skylar replied.

"So, you pitched in college?" Mia changed the subject.

"Yeah. I wanted to pitch for the USA, but the injury happened, and I couldn't. That's why I went as a coach."

"Better than nothing, which is what I have."

"You were on the team as a player," Skylar said as she slowed the car.

"Not in the games," Mia replied.

"Because you left the team," Skylar pulled over and parked. "From what I understand, you would have been the starting pitcher had you stayed. A few of the coaches – and don't tell anyone else this ever – actually told me I had my work cut out for me without you on the team."

"Really?" Mia asked, smiling over at her.

"We have great pitching. Don't get me wrong; we do. But they seemed to believe the sun rose and set with your fastball, Mia Landis." Skylar gave her a wink.

Mia liked that wink.

"Are we here?" she asked.

"Yeah, this is his place." Skylar nodded at the modest house to their right. "Are you ready for those trust falls and team-building activities?" she teased.

"I'm ready to play softball, so if that's what it takes, I say, bring it on," Mia replied.

Skylar's expression changed then. Mia didn't know what she had said, but it appeared to be good, because Skylar's pensive expression from before had dissipated completely. She looked relaxed now and even had the smallest of smiles on her face.

"That's a good answer," the woman said after a long moment.

"What's the bad answer?" Mia asked her, now more than curious.

"Something that would lead me to believe you weren't willing to do what it takes."

"I just moved my entire life to a city I'd never even been to before; uprooting my–"

There was a knock on Mia's window, startling her.

"It's just Stephanie." Skylar laughed. "We should probably go."

"Right," Mia said, turning to see Stephanie smiling and waving at them. She opened the door and said, "You scared the crap out of me."

"I know. It was hilarious," Stephanie replied while laughing.

A moment later, Mia felt Skylar step up beside her and say, "We have a whole weekend of that to look forward to."

"Bring it on," Mia repeated.

Their eyes met, and Mia felt as if maybe she had this woman's respect for the first time since they'd met.

CHAPTER 10

SKYLAR could not get a read on Mia Landis. One second, she's distracted and making phone calls when she should be focused on practice. The next, she talked about bringing it all on because she was willing to do what it took. Currently, Mia was standing over by the grill, talking to Tom as he showed her pictures of his three kids on his phone. Skylar was sitting by Leslie and Jenny, who were talking about their boyfriends and making things work long-distance.

"Sky, you were dating someone, right?" Leslie asked.

Skylar turned back to them and said, "I was, but we broke up."

"You didn't have to move," Jenny said.

"No, but she did," Skylar told her. "She's playing for Boise."

"And you called it quits?" Leslie asked.

"Not because of that. That was probably one reason it happened sooner, but things weren't great before that."

"What was her name again?" Jenny asked.

"Tori. Victoria Ray."

"Tori? I know Tori," Stephanie said as she approached. "She just graduated, didn't she?" She sat down in an empty chair.

"Yeah, she's in Boise now. On the team there," Skylar replied.

"My girlfriend came with me," Stephanie said. "She just graduated, too. She's looking for a job out here now."

"That's nice," Skylar said, trying not to take that as a dig against her failed relationship since she knew distance had not been the cause of their break-up.

"She's great. When I told her I was leaving school early to do this, she totally supported me. And since she was graduating, she said she'd go with me wherever."

"Lucky you," Leslie said.

"Did everyone enjoy their food?" Cheryl asked rather loudly from the middle of Tom's backyard.

There were nods, some cheers, and a few shouts of thank you to Tom for grilling and being a great host.

"Good to hear. Now, you all get to clean up the mess. Tom is going to assign you each a chore. Your task is to work together to achieve all of the chores within the next thirty minutes. If you do this, tonight at the campsite, the coaches will set up all of the tents while the players relax by the fire, and we'll cook you a late dinner."

The team cheered in response to that.

"If not, you all must set up the tents, including the coaches' tents, and cook *us* dinner."

"What are the chores?" one of the players yelled.

"There are close to thirty people here," Cheryl began. "That's a lot of trash and a lot of dishes. Plus, Tom said his lawn needs mowing, and there's a bathroom that needs cleaning."

"I have two boys," Tom added. "They're not particularly neat in the bathroom department."

"I think Tom's wife would like the carpet vacuumed as well," Cheryl said. "So, there are five tasks. Bathroom cleaning, vacuuming, mowing the lawn, doing the dishes, collecting and taking out the trash. All twenty-three players must do at least one task, but you can do more than one to help the team. When I say go, you have thirty minutes. Cleaning supplies are already where they need to be. You all need to band together to strategize the best way to clean up after yourselves."

"And my kids," Tom added with a smile.

"Your first team-building activity starts now. Go!" Cheryl said.

"Well, this is not how I thought I'd be spending my afternoon," Stephanie said.

"I am *not* cleaning that bathroom," Jenny added.

"Me neither," Leslie said, standing up.

Skylar stood and said, "Okay. There's a lot of trash, but it'll be quick. Twenty-three divided by five is four point six. Since we all know how slow Kai is running the bases, she only counts as the point six." Everyone laughed. "Kai and the four to your left are on trash duty." She pointed to the women next to Kai. "Pick it up quickly. Three dish gatherers outside. You, you, and you." She pointed at three other players. "Two dish people inside actually washing and drying until the other three are done out here, and they can help. Two women in the bathroom, since that's about all that will fit. I'll be one of them, since I don't scare easily."

"I'll help," Mia said, raising her hand. "I don't scare easily, either."

Skylar liked that comment.

"There's only one vacuum, is my guess. So, one person, take that. Let's have four others walking around and picking up anything off the floor that we don't want destroyed."

"I've got it," Leslie said. "Who's picking things up for me?"

A few players raised their hands.

"Let's aim higher than just meeting the goal. Only one person can mow the lawn. The rest of you without a job, clean counters, straighten up the chairs out here, do whatever you can in thirty to make Tom's house better than we found it. No offense, Tom," she said.

"None taken," he said.

"All right. Let's go!" Skylar said loudly.

All of the women branched off into their mini-teams. Mia moved closer to Skylar. Skylar watched as everyone went inside the house or otherwise got to work.

"Aiming for team captain?" Mia asked.

"I guess I'm still used to being a coach," she replied.

"I bet you were good at it."

Skylar watched as Mia dropped that compliment and then walked into the house. Skylar followed close behind.

***

"I can honestly say I've never cleaned a bathroom faster," Mia told her later as they sat by the fire at the campsite. "And we still didn't get everything done."

"Well, we didn't know Tom would come through and check the top of the mirror for dust, did we?" Skylar asked, smiling over at Tom, who was very much enjoying watching two players setting up his solo tent for the night.

"Do you think there's a lesson there?" Mia asked.

"Huh?" Skylar turned to her.

"In that, we didn't ask any questions. We just jumped up like little worker bees and started cleaning. We didn't ask what they were looking for or what the goal really was. We didn't think about the dust above the mirror. We probably should have asked for criteria or something."

"I think you're overcomplicating it. Tom just needed to clean the house after we'd all stormed in."

"Maybe," Mia said. Then, her phone buzzed. "Sorry. I have to—"

"Sure." Skylar waved it off.

She watched as Mia stood up from one of the seven horizontal logs sitting around the large fire they had built in the middle.

"You two are in a tent tonight?" Kai asked Skylar, scooting over to her on the log.

"Yeah. Why?"

"Do you think she snores? Jenny just told me *she* snores, and I'm stuck with her. I'm a light sleeper, Sky."

"Sorry." Skylar laughed. "I don't know if she snores. I met her this week, and we didn't exactly talk about sleeping habits on the ride over."

"I thought we weren't supposed to be on our phones." She pointed at Mia, who was talking on hers several yards away.

"I don't think they're going to enforce that. We finished putting up all the tents and cooking the coaches their food. Well, except for Tabby and McGuire, who can't seem to figure out Tom's tent. We're relaxing for the night. I think they'll give her a pass."

"Well, I'm going to go take a shower at that ugly-looking concrete building. It kind of reminds me of my college dorm bathroom. Three toilet stalls. Universal-sink-type situation and not nearly enough showers for the twenty-five women here tonight and the other campers." Jenny stood up. "Then, I'm getting some rest. I'm trying to be smart and go to bed early. I have no idea what they have planned for us this weekend." She walked off.

Skylar decided to do the same and made her way to the tent she would share with Mia tonight. It was just big enough for the two of them. There was a lantern in the corner. She turned it on and rifled through her bag to find the clothes she'd sleep in. She then changed quickly, taking advantage of the empty tent.

"Okay. Thank you for calling. I appreciate it," Mia said.

Skylar couldn't exactly avoid hearing it. Mia must have been right outside the tent now, on her phone. Tents weren't exactly soundproof, so she couldn't be blamed for eavesdropping. The zipper went down. Skylar turned around to see Mia looking in.

"Sorry, just came in to change," she told Mia.

"Oh, I didn't know. I was going to do the same thing," Mia replied.

"I'll leave you to it. I'm going to the bathroom and then turning in for the night."

"Same," Mia said, moving into the tent and sitting down on top of the sleeping bag she had set out for herself earlier.

"Cool. I'll see you in a few then."

Skylar slid out of the tent, made her way to the bathroom, and ran into Mia again on her way out as Mia entered. By the time Mia had finished, Skylar was inside her sleeping bag with her headphones plugged in. She usually listened to music to help her fall asleep. When she was alone at home, she listened without headphones. Whenever Tori had been there, she'd put them in because Tori was a light sleeper who needed complete silence to sleep. Mia slid into her own sleeping bag, making almost no noise, like a stealthy ninja. Skylar had tripped over her own shoes when she had first gotten into the small tent.

"You don't have to wear the headphones," Mia said.

"Huh?" Skylar wasn't sure she had heard correctly.

"Are you listening to music?"

"Yeah," she said, pulling the headphones out of her ears.

"It won't bother me," Mia replied.

"It'll bother me!" The voice belonged to one of the players, likely already in their tent for the night.

"Never mind, then," Mia said, chuckling.

"You listen to music when you go to sleep?" Skylar asked.

"No, but I'm used to noise." Mia tucked herself into the sleeping bag a little farther. "This place is kind of quiet, with the exception of the crickets."

"You didn't bring headphones?"

"No, I didn't even think about it."

Skylar looked at her own hands, making a choice. Then, she held one of the earbuds out to Mia.

"Here. If you can stand what I have on my phone, you can listen with me," she told her.

"No, it's okay. I don't want to–"

"Mia, just take the thing. I'll fall asleep in, like, twenty minutes anyway. Right before I fall asleep, I always turn it off."

"Okay. If you're sure, that would be nice." Mia took the earbud from her.

"We might have to…" Skylar moved a little closer to Mia. "I don't have the Bluetooth ones yet. I might want to invest." She slid the earbud into her own ear as Mia did the same, scooting a little closer to Skylar.

"We don't have—"

"It's fine. You ready?" she asked, cutting Mia off.

"Sure."

Skylar pressed play on her phone, turning her body to face Mia at the same time. Mia continued to lie flat on her back, staring up at the ceiling of their tent.

"Is this okay?" Skylar asked.

"I'm not judging your taste in music, if that's what you're asking," Mia replied, turning her face to her.

Skylar realized they hadn't turned off the lantern yet, but she wasn't sure she wanted to now. Mia was perfectly lit in this moment. Mia's bright-green eyes glowed now with flecks of gold in them. Her nose was small for her face but was somehow also just right. Her eyelashes were long. Skylar had the urge to kiss them in that moment as Mia blinked rapidly. Mia licked her lips. Skylar squinted at her, wondering if Mia knew what she was doing, or she did it subconsciously, or just had dry lips she needed to address.

Skylar rolled onto her own back. She did not need to be looking at another player that way. She needed to remain focused her game, focused on whether or not Mia could be a fit for the national team, and focusing on the first season of this new league. She did not need to be thinking about how beautiful Mia Landis was as they lay next to one another in a tent at some lame team-building event.

CHAPTER 11

"SHE'S still got a fever?" Mia asked quietly into the phone.

"She's a little warm. I checked her temperature. She's at ninety-eight point nine. It's nothing to worry about. I gave her another dose of her medicine. She's a little lethargic, though, which is why I called. Is she normally hard to wake up in the morning?"

"She's a deep sleeper. I'm luckier than most parents."

"There you go. Nothing to worry about then. She's probably just still waking up for the day. I'll keep a close eye on her. If she doesn't start feeling better soon, I'll call you back, and we can see about getting her to the urgent care nearby or if—"

"Urgent care?" Mia asked a little louder than she'd planned.

"Everything okay?" Skylar approached, carrying two cups of fire-brewed coffee.

"Everything's fine. I just need a second," Mia replied, turning around away from her.

"Okay. I brought you coffee. I guess I'll just leave it outside the tent so bugs can crawl in it," Skylar muttered sarcastically.

"Is she really okay?" Mia asked into the phone.

"She'll be fine, dear. I promise, I will let you know if there's anything to worry about."

"Okay. I can be home in an hour. I didn't drive myself, so I might need—"

"Don't hop in the car just yet. I'll call you if I think you need to get back, okay?"

"Okay," Mia replied, not convincing even herself that staying with the team right now was the right decision.

She disconnected the phone just in time to turn around and see Skylar placing the coffee on the dirt just outside the tent.

"I'll leave you alone," Skylar said as she stood to see Mia was now off the phone.

"I'm sorry. I didn't mean to be short with you," Mia said.

"No big deal. I was trying to do something nice for you; team-building and all that. But I can see I chose the wrong moment."

"Skylar, I—"

"Is everything okay?" she interrupted. "You can tell me if something's up. I won't tell anyone."

Mia sighed and said, "It's not a big secret or anything, but I'm trying to figure out how to balance all of this. It's just a lot all at once, and I'm doing it on my own."

"Doing what all on your own? Joining the team? Moving?"

"I have a daughter, Skylar."

"You do?"

"It's why I left the national team, to begin with," Mia said. "I got pregnant."

"Right," Skylar replied, looking over Mia's shoulder for some reason before meeting Mia's eyes again. "You're a mom. Makes sense why you're distracted sometimes. What's her name?" Skylar took a drink of her coffee.

"Hazel. I named her after my grandmother." Mia smiled.

"Pretty name."

"Thank you," Mia replied, picking up the coffee Skylar had brought her to take a drink, feeling the warmth rush over her instantly. "I don't do well in the cold." She took another sip. "Thank you for this."

"Well, you didn't exactly dress for camping." Skylar pointed at her. "You're wearing sweats."

"What was I supposed to wear?" Mia asked.

"It doesn't get crazy cold here most nights, but it's always better in these sleeping bags, which are made for the cold nights, to just sleep in your underwear."

"Did *you* sleep in your underwear?" Mia asked, gulping and taking another sip to, hopefully, cover that gulp up.

"Yeah. Well, I slept in a sports bra and my underwear. I thought you would have noticed." She gave a slight smirk.

"You were in the sleeping bag already," Mia replied, giving her a slight smirk in return.

Why had she done that? Why had she smirked back at her? Stop smirking, she told herself silently.

"I got in wearing clothes and took them off after. Sweats will just make sure you never get warm. Do you have any thermal underwear or anything made for camping?"

"No. I'm not much for camping," Mia replied. "I was kind of hoping to never have to go camping in my life."

"I've been a bunch, but I grew up in the middle of nowhere. There's not much to do, so sometimes, you just pack some crap and go into the woods for a few days. I have an extra pair. We're about the same size. You can borrow them. That should help." Skylar took a few steps toward her, and with her free hand, she reached out and slid it up and down Mia's arm rapidly. "And maybe a thermal undershirt, too. I have one. This isn't cold to me. Let me grab both for you. I'll lay them out and give you some time to change. That should help."

"You don't have to–"

"I'm not letting our starting pitcher freeze to death, Mia. We haven't even played our first game yet."

Mia nodded, accepting that Skylar was just looking out for the team.

"Well, I'd appreciate it. Thank you."

"If you need to call your boyfriend or husband back, I'll leave you alone."

"What?" Mia asked.

"I didn't know who you were talking to before. I don't

see you wearing a ring, but we don't when we play, so I–"

"Oh. That was my babysitter," Mia told her. "She's watching Hazel while we're here. I just met her, and I don't like leaving my kid with someone I just met, but I wasn't expecting a weekend trip so soon. We have a few weeks before the first away games, and I thought I'd have more time to build my daycare network. Hazel had a little fever yesterday. She's still pretty warm. I'm just trying to figure out how much trouble I'll get in if I have to leave this thing early. If she gets worse, I'll need a ride from someone, so that means two people are leaving early, and I–"

"Mia." That hand moved to Mia's arm again. "It's your kid. Cheryl and the others will understand. If she's sick, and you have to go – you have to go. It would suck for you to miss this stuff, but people would understand."

"Would you?" Mia asked with a genuine interest in Skylar's answer.

"Because I gave you a hard time about being distracted?"

"Yeah."

"I won't lie to you. This season – this chance to play again – is the most important thing in my life right now. It's all I care about. I guess I do wish that were true for everyone here, because that would make us all focused on this and only this, but I can't expect everyone else to feel the same way I do. I mean, one of the reasons my girlfriend and I broke up recently was because of that. It wasn't the only reason – I'm not that petty, but it was one of them." She sighed loudly and removed her hand from Mia's arm. "Anyway... I want a family of my own someday. When I have it, *that* will be the most important thing in the world to me. Softball is my life now, but it won't always be. I get it."

Had Mia heard her right? Had she said *girlfriend?*

"Thank you," Mia said, deciding not to focus on that topic just yet.

"We have a morning run in five minutes. Everyone,

get ready!" Tom yelled over the grouping of tents.

Mia dressed for the run after Skylar did the same. When Mia entered the tent after Skylar had gone, she noticed the thermal shirt and pants set out on her sleeping bag. She wouldn't need them for the run, but she'd be grateful for them later. The run was three miles on one of the less popular hiking trails. Three miles one way, more specifically. That also meant three miles back. Mia was in shape, but she hadn't run six miles in a long time. And she had never run six miles on a bumpy hiking trail. She caught herself nearly tripping a few times. The last time, they had just emerged from the woods. The run was over. They'd walk from the parking lot back to their campsite as their cool down. That's when Mia tripped over a rock on the concrete. In slow motion, she saw herself falling to the hard ground. Her hands flew out on instinct, to save her face from the surface, but before she hit it, there were two arms wrapping around her back from behind, pulling her up.

"I've got you," Skylar said as Mia stabilized.

"Thanks. I didn't see that rock there."

"Listen up, Number One. You need to make it through the season unscathed if we have any chance of bringing home some victories. Can you make sure you don't kill yourself first?" Skylar let go of Mia and chuckled at her.

"Number One?" Mia asked.

"Starting pitcher." Skylar moved to stand beside her. She didn't look like she had a drop of sweat on her, while Mia was drowning in it. "You get number one. So, I'm calling you Number One from now on."

"My number is three. I've always worn number three," Mia replied with a lifted eyebrow.

"Number One has a much nicer ring to it, though, doesn't it, Number One?"

Mia laughed. They walked back to the site together with neither of them saying anything of consequence. When they made it back, it was time for a break and some lunch. The players made sandwiches, and there were chips. They ate at the picnic tables surrounding the site. Mia sat down next to Jenny, wanting to get to know the other pitcher on the team as much as she could, as well as Kai, the other catcher. Skylar would likely be the starter, but if she needed a break, or got injured again, Mia would be working with Kai. Skylar was sitting at another table, laughing along with the three players surrounding her as if she were an actor on a stage. She'd say something. They'd all laugh.

"She's the life of the party," Jenny said.

"Who is?" Mia asked.

"Sky. I hadn't seen her in a while before this league thing popped up, but I know she wasn't happy just being a coach. She's a lot happier now. And when she's happy, she's the life of the party and a big-time flirt."

"Flirt?"

"Not with anyone here, though. She wouldn't date teammates," Jenny replied.

"She takes the sport way too seriously for that," Kai added, taking a bite of her ham and cheese sandwich. "She just ended a relationship basically because of that."

"It wasn't *because* of that. Don't start rumors," Jenny told her. Then, she looked over at Mia. "Sky said it was over before that. Tori making the Boise team just made it a little bit easier."

"Her ex is a player?" Mia asked.

"Yeah, Victoria Ray. She's nothing to write home about, if you ask me," Kai said.

"She's a good player, but I don't think she's pro league material," Jenny agreed.

"I heard from one of the players on Boise, that I went to college with, that Tori wasn't even going to play. She wanted to go to grad school. She had gotten in somewhere but turned it down because it was out of state, and she didn't want to be that far from Sky. She was going to reapply to some in-state schools and just get a job or something. Apparently, she wanted to move in with Sky, but Sky wasn't ready. I guess, when the writing was on the wall, Tori decided to try out, and she made the Boise Stingers."

"What did I just say about starting rumors?" Jenny asked.

"It's not a rumor. It's what Tori told my friend. Why would she make that up?"

Mia looked back toward Skylar, who stood up and said something Mia couldn't make out. Alex Samford, the backup to the backup pitcher on their roster and, likely, starting center fielder, stood up with her, brushed Skylar's shoulder with her hand, and laughed at whatever had been said. Skylar, for what it was worth, looked a little taken aback by the gesture but smiled at Alex all the same. Mia glared.

"Mia, what are your national team plans?" Kai asked her, bringing Mia back to their conversation.

"National team?"

"Yeah, you're back in the game, right? I just assumed you'd want to make the roster for Paris," Kai replied.

"Oh, I don't know. I wasn't even sure I'd make a team here. I just want to focus on getting back into the game and playing the best I can with you guys. I'll worry about the other stuff later."

She found herself looking back at Skylar yet again. It was a new thing for her. She couldn't remember a time where she needed – not wanted, but *needed* – to know where someone was like this. As she watched Skylar take a drink from her water bottle, she noticed the tank top the woman had worn for the run, tightening around her abdominal muscles. Mia swallowed. She had never really ogled a woman like this before, and that was exactly what she was doing right now. She wasn't sure she had ever even looked at Francesca like this before. Her attraction to her hadn't been just physical. It hadn't even been a physical attraction at all, at first; it was more intellectual.

She had been dealing with Gregg's declining interest in just about everything, including but not limited to sex. Talking to Francesca, at first, had been more a relief. She had found someone to confide in and who she also happened to enjoy being around. Maybe it was because Mia hadn't always known about her attraction to women that her reaction to Francesca was different than her current reaction to Skylar Donahue. She watched as Skylar reached down to scratch her stomach under her shirt and thought about how nice it would be to grasp that hem and pull that shirt over Skylar's head.

She had been with two women in her life. Both of them had been one-night stands. Mia wasn't ashamed of that. It was what she had needed at the time, and it had helped her figure out more about who she was and what she wanted, now that her marriage was coming to an end. She had also been with one man during that time. He had not been her type and had been underwhelming in the bedroom department. One of the women had also been a bit of a dud, causing Mia to fake an orgasm just to make her feel better. She knew she shouldn't have done it, but she had. She wasn't proud of that. With the second woman, though, she hadn't had to fake anything.

Mia had met her in a bar. She'd been charming and sexy as hell. She had kissed Mia about fifteen minutes after meeting her, and it had been a good kiss; good enough that Mia let the woman take her home. The sex had been outstanding, but Mia knew she had just met a player who was only interested in that. That worked for Mia, though. She had enjoyed her night, and she had enjoyed that woman.

Right now, though, as Mia stared at Skylar, she realized she had thought that woman was sexy, but that she hadn't pictured herself yanking off her clothes that night. She hadn't thought about what it would be like to kiss her, before the woman had leaned in and taken away the chance to wonder. Skylar looked her way just as Mia licked her lips. She watched as Skylar's eyebrows lifted and then lowered. The expression on her face changed to that of confusion. Mia looked away.

CHAPTER 12

MIA HAD been giving her glances a lot this weekend, which both intrigued Skylar and confused her. The woman was annoying that way. It had been a long day, and Skylar was tired. She was probably just reading too much into the fact that every time she looked Mia's way, Mia was looking at her. Of course, she hadn't stopped to think about the fact that she was looking over herself, which is why she noticed Mia glancing back at her. She slid off her t-shirt and her pants once in her sleeping bag and tossed them next to her. She was more than ready for sleep. It was, thankfully, their last night sleeping on the campsite ground. Skylar wanted her comfortable queen bed at home, with its relatively new mattress and the special pillows she'd bought in order to sleep better on her side.

"Can I come in?" Mia's voice came from outside the tent.

"Yeah, I'm good," Skylar replied.

She wasn't sure why she cared so much. She was an athlete. So was Mia. They had both seen plenty of naked women in locker rooms. But, for some reason, the thought of Mia seeing her naked or nearly naked just because she was changing her clothes, didn't seem right. Mia unzipped the tent and lowered herself to enter. Then, she put her toiletry kit into her duffel bag and moved to slide into the sleeping bag next to Skylar. Skylar pretended to be readying her headphones but looked sideways as Mia removed her shirt and pants while safely tucked away.

"I'm exhausted," Mia said. Then, she reached for her phone and glanced at the screen. "What about you?"

"I'm okay," she lied. "Everything okay with your daughter?"

"She's better." Mia looked over at her and smiled. "The medicine helped."

"I'm glad." Skylar smiled back, rolling on her side to face her. "So, how are you liking our little team-building getaway so far?"

"I wish I would have had a little more time to prepare. I haven't even moved into my apartment completely yet." Mia rolled to face Skylar. "Plus, I didn't know it would be this hard to be away from her. I had to travel for the try-outs, but that was the first time I'd been without her since she was born. She was with my mom back home, so I wasn't nearly as worried as I am now."

"How old is she?"

"She's two," Mia replied. "Going on thirty."

"We're about the same age, then. I'm twenty-five, going on thirty," Skylar teased with a smile.

"I *am* thirty, and I feel like I'm thirty going on fifty. I never really felt old until I was at those try-outs, and then again, sitting on those bleachers that first day with the team. All the girls saying they'd either left school or had just graduated, and I feel like I should be retiring, not joining a new league."

"Retiring? Are you crazy?" Skylar asked.

"I did leave."

"Because you wanted a family. A lot of female pro athletes do that, and a lot of them come back."

"It's not just that," Mia said, reaching for the earbud Skylar held out for her.

"What is it then?" Skylar tucked her own into her ear.

"There was just a lot going on in my personal life. I didn't think I could give one hundred percent to the team, which wasn't fair to them. I still worry now that I can't give that to this team. I probably should have just stayed home, coaching and teaching PE. Hazel would have had more stability then."

"If you feel that way, what made you try out?" Skylar asked.

"I had a couple of people in my corner telling me to do it *for* Hazel. When she grows up, I want to be able to not just tell her to go for her dreams but to be able to tell her that I did, too."

"And what's your dream, specifically?"

"I'd imagine it's the same one you have. I want to play in the Olympics. Ever since I was a kid, it's what I've dreamed of. Nothing ever compared to that."

"Same for me," Skylar said with a smile.

"You've at least been."

"As a coach. It's not the same. Don't get me wrong; it was amazing. But I want the whole experience as a player. I want to walk in the opening ceremony, rocking that kick-ass Ralph Lauren gear." She laughed a little. "And wave that American flag. I want to take the field in uniform and play in the gold medal game, stand on the podium, hearing my national anthem, and celebrate after like the Women's World Cup team after they repeated as champs."

Mia laughed and said, "They did celebrate. I think some of them were drunk for four straight days."

"Well, they earned it. I don't so much plan on being drunk, but I want to pop the champagne cork with my teammates and celebrate the hard work and sacrifices it takes to get that far."

"Does it bother you that you won't be pitching?" Mia asked.

"Yeah." Her mouth formed a straight line. "I'd be lying if I said I dreamed of being in the games as a catcher. I'd planned on pitching a no-hitter."

"Obviously," Mia replied.

"But I'd be just as happy to be the catcher of your no-hitter if it means we're bringing home a medal," Skylar said.

"Yeah?"

"Yeah. I chose a team sport for a reason, Mia. It's not all about me."

"Seemed like it was earlier today at lunch," Mia replied with a lifted eyebrow.

"Huh?" Skylar wasn't sure what she was talking about.

"You were, to quote Jenny, *'the life of the party.'*"

"Oh, I was telling them the story of how one of the busses broke down for the Worlds, and how we all decided to get out of the bus and have a dance party in the middle of nowhere while it got fixed. I guess they thought that was funny."

"Samford seemed to be interested." Mia turned to face the top of the tent.

"Can I ask you something?" Skylar decided to risk it.

"Sure."

"Before, when you told me the babysitter was on the phone, you conveniently didn't answer the question about a boyfriend or a husband."

"So, your question is whether or not I have one?" Mia turned her face back to Skylar.

"Yeah."

"I don't," she replied.

"Okay." Skylar rolled this time.

She wanted to ask something else, but she didn't.

"Okay," Mia said. "Sleep?"

"Music?"

"Sure," Mia replied.

"Great," Skylar said and started up the music.

***

They repeated their run from the previous day, ate lunch, and then sat around talking, telling stories about their very first softball seasons as kids, their roughest games, harshest defeats, and the lessons they learned from them. Skylar thought it was an effective activity for them all to get to know each other, but by the time the cars were packed up, she was more than ready to head home.

"Are you ready?" Skylar asked Mia.

"Yeah, I loaded up the trunk."

"Thanks," Skylar said, climbing behind the wheel. "It's nearly dinner time. If you want, we can stop and grab something on the way back."

"Oh, I would, but I need to get home. I have to pick up my car and then go get Hazel from the babysitter's place." Mia buckled her seat belt.

"If it's on the way, I don't mind stopping and picking her up, too."

"Car seat," Mia said, hooking a thumb toward the backseat.

"Oh, right. I didn't think about that," Skylar said, feeling like an idiot. "Well, I'll just take you home, then."

"I'm sure you have better things to do than deal with a tired kid and her exhausted mother even for a brief car ride." Mia chuckled as she looked over at Skylar.

"You'd be surprised," Skylar replied.

They drove in relative silence. Every so often, one of them would make a comment about the song on the radio or on the weekend's activities, but for the most part, Mia was quiet, choosing to stare out the side window at the scenery passing by.

"You spent time here as part of the national team, right?" Skylar asked just as they pulled off the highway.

"Yeah. Why?"

"You're just looking out the window like you've never seen anything like it before."

"Oh, sorry. I think the exhaustion is just catching up to me. I had the try-outs. Then, the team I was coaching was in the playoffs. I had to move here. It's been a lot. You got lucky. You got placed on the team in your backyard."

"I guess so," Skylar said, turning when the light changed from red to green.

"I'm sorry. I guess maybe it doesn't feel that way to you." Mia turned her body toward Skylar.

"Why would you say that?"

"The rumor mill was working hard this weekend," Mia

said, giving her a sideways smile. "Your girlfriend left when she made another team."

"Yeah, that's the one I mentioned to you before." Skylar glanced over at her. "It wasn't over because of that, though. Is that what people are saying?"

"Some of them."

"Well, fuck." Skylar laughed a little. "Tori plays for Boise now."

"We play them first."

"I know. *That* should be fun," Skylar replied.

"How long were you two together?"

"About two years," Skylar answered honestly. "She's younger than me. She just turned twenty-two. We started dating before I got hurt. It worked for a while, and then it didn't."

"I guess that's all relationships that don't end in forever, huh?" Mia asked.

"I guess so," Skylar pulled into Mia's apartment complex parking lot. "I loved her once, but there were a lot of differences. When I got hurt, I struggled figuring out what was next for me. She was supportive as hell, and she didn't deserve me ending things, but it just didn't feel right anymore. When she told me she was trying out, I actually got upset because this was supposed to be my thing. She played in college because she got a scholarship, not because it was her dream." Skylar sighed out her embarrassment. "Then, I thought about how it might actually be a good thing. If she makes a team, it wouldn't likely be the one I was on, assuming I made one, too."

"It would give you an excuse to end it," Mia said.

"Not an excuse, but it did make things ending between us easier. She had to move pretty immediately. I stayed here." She pulled up in front of Mia's building. "Anyway, that's the story. It didn't end because of the league. I fell out of love with Tori. That's why it ended. The league thing is more about *when* it ended. It probably saved us a bunch of fights, and that whole being-way-too-close-to-your-ex thing lesbians deal with a lot." She chuckled. "It usually causes problems when one of you starts dating again. Now, I don't have to worry about that." Skylar glanced over at Mia. "I guess you wouldn't have any idea what I'm talking about, though, would you?"

"Being close friends with your ex? No, I definitely don't understand that," Mia replied.

"I'm sure it's not as bad for the straights, but for ladies who love ladies, and especially in the city we live in –which is more of a small town where lesbians are concerned – it's pretty prevalent. I have a friend that's gotten back together with her ex-girlfriend three times. They date other people and just always seem to go back to each other."

Mia didn't say anything for a minute. She just stared over at Skylar, who stared back at her. A strange moment passed between them; one where it kind of felt like Skylar was dropping Mia off at the end of a date. Mia bit her bottom lip as if she wanted to say something but decided against it instead.

"I should go. I have to pick Hazel up in twenty minutes, or the sitter charges me extra."

"Hey, do you have another job lined up out here?" Skylar asked, realizing in that moment that she hadn't already.

"Not yet. Why?" Mia opened the car door.

"The coaching jobs that are left are going to go fast. If you haven't applied already, you should. But I have a lead on something else if you're interested."

"You don't need it?"

"Not right now, no," Skylar answered. "There's a softball little league that just lost its vice president to a higher-paying gig, is my guess. Anyway, they play down the street from our field. It's administrative, but I'm sure you'd be a good fit for it. It's not a full-time job, and they're pretty good with flexible schedules. I had a player friend who worked for them last year. I could put in a good word."

"That would be amazing," Mia replied. "But, why me?

There are twenty-one other girls on this team."

"They'll be fine," Skylar said.

"It's because I'm a mom, isn't it?" Mia asked.

"Just accept the offer, Mia." Skylar laughed. "I'll call them tomorrow and let them know you're interested. You take it from there. If it works out, great."

"Thanks, Skylar. I really appreciate it."

"You know everyone calls me Sky, right? You can do that, too."

"Okay. Sky." Mia hesitated as if trying to see how it sounded coming out of her mouth. "Thank you."

CHAPTER 13

AFTER a short two weeks of practice, the team was about to play its first set of games. Mia's shoulder was holding up well, which was a good sign. Skylar's wrist appeared to be okay, but she did put it in that brace whenever they weren't practicing, which made Mia concerned. She had broached the subject once, earned a scowl, and never brought it up again. It was Skylar's injury to manage, but if it interfered with the team's success, Mia would bring it up again.

The Boise Stingers were coming to town for a set of three games. Then, the Boomers would go to Cincinnati for three away games to play the Stars. It would be back and forth like that for the next couple of months. Luckily, Mia had found the right daycare and weekend care for Hazel, including the few nights she would be gone at away games. She had also gotten that job, thanks to Skylar putting in a good word for her. She would work two days a week in the office, and when she was away, she could work remotely or just make the days up when she got back. Most of the people working there were part-time or volunteers, so it really was the perfect job for her right now. It didn't pay well, but it, combined with her player salary, would pay enough.

Skylar laughed and said, "You can't leave now. We just got here."

"I have to pick Hazel up," Mia replied.

They'd practiced hard that day. Then, they'd all iced their weary muscles, and just as Mia had been about to leave, a few of the players had mentioned wanting to go out for drinks. Mia didn't want to drink, but she was starting to enjoy being a part of a team again. She missed this comradery and thought that hanging out for a bit wouldn't hurt. They'd gone to a bar a few minutes away from the practice field. She had chosen to have water instead of alcohol, as had Skylar, but the other four players in the group had opted for beer.

"Come on. Stay another few minutes," Skylar encouraged. "If the sitter charges you extra, I'll pay for it. You wouldn't let me buy you a drink."

"Look who's talking. You have water, too."

"I'm driving. I like to be careful."

"So am I, and so *do* I," Mia said, laughing.

"Fine. Fine. But if you're going now, you have to stay twice as long next time," Skylar said.

"What? That's ridiculous," Mia replied, finishing the water in her glass and crunching on an ice cube.

She didn't actually want to go. She was just used to saying that she *had* to go. Hanging out with the team was fun. Getting to know Skylar better over the last couple of weeks had also been fun. Well, more than fun, technically.

One night, she'd gone out into the living room after Hazel had fallen asleep. She had closed the bedroom door behind her, turned on the TV to try to drown out the sound, and turned her vibrator on its lowest setting. Then, she had closed her eyes and tried to think of Francesca or that one-night stand that had been life-changing, but instead, she could only picture Skylar Donahue. Images flashed through her mind of Skylar in the locker room, where they sometimes showered after workouts or practice.

Mia hadn't seen Skylar in anything less than a towel, but it was enough to make her press that vibrator down against her clit a little harder. She had pictured Skylar between her legs, on top of her, driving into her, under her, with Mia returning the favor, and in just about every other position. She'd come that night, whispering Skylar's name. And she now had a problem; more than one, actually. One problem had to do with her new nightly activity. Put Hazel to sleep, grab the vibrator, and get off thinking about Skylar's hands all over her own body. The other problem had to do with the fact that it was Skylar doing the touching.

She could not and should not be having sex fantasies about a teammate.

Skylar was staring at her now with those light-gray eyes and cocky smile, and Mia wanted to lean over and kiss that cocky smile off her damn face. She couldn't, though. She'd never, in her life, had feelings for another player like this. Even if she quit the team tomorrow, Skylar wasn't right for her; she dated younger women. Younger women who hadn't given birth and now had a two-year-old at home that required Mia's love, devotion, and care.

"Sky, how are you dealing with Tori coming back?" Gaby asked.

"What?" Skylar turned her attention from Mia to Gaby.

"Tori. She's here for the next few days, right?"

"For the games, yeah," Skylar replied.

"Have you talked to her since she left?"

"No. She came by to pick up her stuff. That was it." She shrugged.

"You two were together for a long time, and nothing?" Leslie asked.

"It was two years. In the grand scheme of things, that's not all that long." Skylar finished her water. "And no, we haven't talked. We're both moving on. That's what you do when you break up with someone." She then glanced at Mia. "I'm going to get home. Walk you out?"

"Sure," Mia replied.

She wasn't sure if the change in conversation had been the cause, but Skylar wanted to leave now. Mia stood up and said her goodbyes to the rest of the group. Then, she followed Skylar out the door and into the parking lot.

"I'll see you tomorrow," Skylar said.

"Are you okay?" Mia asked.

"Yeah. Why?"

"You seemed fine until they brought up your ex-girlfriend. Are you okay with her coming back?"

"I'm just tired of everyone bringing it up. My

relationship history seems to be of constant amusement or concern for half the team. I'd rather they all be focused on winning, and not on the fact that Tori is on the other team, and we used to date."

"For what it's worth, I don't think they mean it like that."

"I know. They're not bad people. It's just annoying. And I'd rather be worrying about how much your fastball hurts my hand when it smacks into my glove than about my ex-girlfriend. I mean, she probably already has a new girlfriend by now, anyway."

"It hurts when it hits your hand?" Mia asked, lifting an eyebrow at her.

Skylar smiled and said, "See? That's what I mean. Thank you for focusing on the game and not my love life."

"Well, from what you've told me, you don't have one to talk about," Mia teased.

"Touché." Skylar laughed and played with the keys in her hand.

"But, seriously, it hurts your hand?"

"Yes," Skylar replied, still laughing. "I'm just glad it's my other wrist that's messed up, or I wouldn't be able to catch for you. I'd have to pair up with Jenny, who throws more off-speed stuff."

"Should I slow down for you?" Mia asked, taking a step toward her.

Skylar thought about something and said, "Probably."

It was a serious answer to a not serious question that was actually masking the serious one Mia hadn't meant to ask. Mia swallowed and stood still. Skylar looked down at the keys in her hand and then back up to Mia.

"I should get some sleep," she said after a long moment.

"And I have to go pick up my kid," Mia replied.

"Right. Hazel." Skylar nodded as if just now remembering that Mia had a daughter. "Tell her hi for me. Wait. She doesn't even know me. Also, she's two years old.

What *do* two-year-olds know? Like, does she remember people after she–"

"You don't spend a lot of time around kids, do you?" Mia laughed.

"Just the grown-up ones who tease me about my ex and how my hand hurts when a certain fastball smacks into it."

Mia smiled and said, "I'll see you tomorrow."

"You too."

***

Mia put her daughter to sleep, which was one of her favorite things to do. She really did feel lucky. Hazel was such a good kid. Mia really had no clue how Gregg could just sign her away like that, but she was grateful for it. It made everything so much easier. As Mia sat on the sofa, she thought about how much happier she had been since she had moved. Things were harder, that was certain, but she was happier, and she hoped Hazel was happier, too.

She reached over to the table where she'd placed her vibrator before sitting down, moved to lie instead, and slid her hand into her shorts. Just thinking about how sexy Skylar was tonight, at the bar, had her wet already. Skylar had changed out of her practice gear and into these dark jeans and a V-neck t-shirt that gave Mia the tiniest hint of cleavage. Skylar's light-brown hair had been down – which it rarely was, and it was a little wavy. Mia pictured herself running her hands through it as she used one hand to stroke herself and the other to try to turn on the vibrator.

She then slid it between her legs and let it take over doing the work for her. She thought about Skylar kissing her neck, her breasts, and moving lower. Her phone pinged, but she ignored it. She returned her thoughts to the only woman who seemed to be able to get her going these days, and came silently a few minutes later. She'd gotten very good at that after Hazel came into the picture.

After she gave herself a bit longer to come down, Mia reached for her phone and saw the email that had come in.

"Shit," she whispered, sitting up.

The email was from the national team. She was on a shortlist of players they were interested in seeing play in an upcoming tournament. Mia stared at the email, couldn't believe what she was reading, and thought about replying right away, but decided against it. She didn't want to appear too eager. Megan Kitchens herself was emailing her. That was a big deal. Mia wasn't sure what had brought on the email, though. They hadn't even played a game yet, but it didn't matter. If she played well, as the email said, they would call her back up for the tournament.

She went to sleep that night smiling. This was what she'd hoped for. She hadn't anticipated it happening all at once, but she could handle it. Being on the national team did come with a paycheck. It was a very small one, but it would help. Regardless, playing for her country wasn't something she needed money for. She would do it for free if they told her that was the only choice.

CHAPTER 14

"REALLY?" Skylar asked.

"You're ready, aren't you?" Megan asked back.

"Yes, I'm ready." She leaned forward in her chair. "But what about the best two catchers in the world you talked about before?"

"One of them is sitting out the tournament. The other one is rehabbing a knee, but it's nothing long-term, only precautionary. Knees are pretty important to catchers." She winked. "Anyway, we need two more for the upcoming NORCECA event. That Wyatt Wicked has been a force for female athletes. It's normally only a volleyball thing, but she's been working with other leagues for female sports to get them to host North, Central America, and Caribbean events just like they do for volleyball. Softball is up first with the NORCECA Softball Championship. It's not a qualifier event, but it might be next time. We've already made it past the initial rounds of qualification, and now, we're in the final tournament. It's a five-day event with eight countries still in the running. They're doing it every other year for now. If we win this one, we'll automatically make the final round for the next one, which will be right before the games. It's a pretty big deal." Megan paused. "I've got most of my players already lined up. I need a new catcher, a couple of pitchers, and a really good power-hitter. You'd be my catcher."

"And Mia is one of the pitchers?" she asked.

"I emailed her last night. She responded this morning."

"Playing hard to get, I see." Skylar laughed lightly and leaned back in her chair again.

"Is she really still that good?"

"Like I told you, she might be better. Her fastball is crazy good, Megan, but she has everything else, too. Plus, she can hit."

"She always could. She was over three hundred before she retired," Megan replied.

"Well, I don't have stats yet, but I've seen her swing in batting practice. She's good."

"Already paying off as a scout." Megan nodded. "And the season hasn't even started yet."

"I'll let you know if anyone else seems of interest to you," she said, standing up.

"And I'll get the paperwork over to you for the tourney, but, Sky, make sure you're ready. If you're not, it's okay to pass on this one."

"What if there's not another one, though?" she asked herself more than Megan.

***

"I thought I should come over and say hi before the game," Tori said.

"How have you been?" Skylar asked her as she adjusted the shin guards of her catcher's gear while sitting in the dugout.

"Good. You?" Tori reached through the chain-link of the fence separating them and leaned forward a bit.

"Good," Skylar said.

"This isn't awkward at all." The woman laughed. "We dated for two years, Sky. We should be able to have a conversation."

"We did just break up. I think this is par for the course," Skylar replied.

"I guess." Tori stared into Skylar's eyes. "I miss you, Sky."

"I miss you, too," she admitted.

"You do?" Tori asked.

"Just because we broke up, doesn't mean I don't miss you, Tor. We didn't work as a couple, but that doesn't mean we can't be friends."

"We disagree about that." The woman pulled back from the fence.

"About being friends?" Skylar looked around to see if any of the coaches or players could overhear, but everyone was already on the field and, likely, out of earshot.

"About us not working as a couple. I thought we did work. You didn't."

"Tor, we agreed that—"

"We agreed to break up because you weren't in love with me anymore, Sky. That doesn't mean I'm not still in love with you. It's been a few weeks, not a few years."

"Hey, did you get it fixed?" Mia asked as she practically jumped into the dugout, looking all adorable in her blue and white uniform.

"Yeah, the strap just got stuck." Skylar held up the shin guard. "Mia, this is Tori. Tori, this is our starting pitcher, Mia Landis."

Mia's eyes got big as she turned her head to Tori and said, "It's nice to meet you." She then looked back at Skylar. "And I should leave you to it. I'm ready to warm up, though, whenever you are."

"Pretty eager there, Number One. Don't wear yourself out before the game even starts."

"Oh, it takes a lot to wear me out, Donahue." Mia winked at Skylar, which caused Skylar to laugh. Then, Mia looked back at Tori and continued, "But I can give you a minute."

"Thanks. I'll be right out," Skylar replied.

Mia waved at Tori awkwardly, turned, and walked out of the dugout back to the bullpen that was just a mound of dirt out in the right field.

"I guess I'll talk to you later, then."

"Huh?" Skylar asked, turning back to Tori.

"Did you just check out her ass?" Tori asked.

"What? No."

"Are you two–"

"Mia and me?" Skylar put the shin guard on her leg. "Tori, come on."

"Don't Tori me. You just flirted with her. Real classy, Sky. I'm standing right here."

"I teased her. She teased me back. Teasing isn't flirting."

"It is the way you do it." Tori turned back to her team. "Doesn't matter. You're single, right?"

"Tor, come on," Skylar said, standing up.

"I've got to go. We're taking the field for warm-ups."

Skylar watched as Tori hustled to her own dugout. Then, she turned to see Mia standing next to Jenny and Kai. Mia looked over at Tori, watching the woman rush off to her own team. Then, Mia looked at Skylar, who smiled at her for some reason. Mia looked down at her glove.

Two hours later, it was the bottom of the seventh and final inning. The Boomers were up by three with one out. Mia was still on the mound, having struck out nine batters. She was also working on a no-hitter, which was crazy. It was the first game of the year. Most players were still working out the kinks in their game, and Mia had been retired as of a few weeks ago. The Stingers had their third baseman at the plate, working a three-two count. Skylar did not like the ever-tightening strike zone this umpire was using. The last two balls he had called would have been strikes with any other ump. She called for a low and outside fastball, and Mia hit the target. The batter swung and missed. Now, there were two outs. One batter and one easy grounder to second base later, and the Boomers had won the first of three games they would play against the Stingers.

After hands were shaken around home plate, Skylar took off her catcher's gear and watched as Mia received a high-five from Jenny and Cheryl for the no-hitter she'd thrown. Mia already had ice on her shoulder, which was a good thing. Skylar knew Cheryl would start Mia every game if she could, so Mia needed to rest that arm.

"Hey, can we talk?" Tori asked, approaching from behind her.

"That depends. Are you going to accuse me of flirting with someone right in front of you?"

"Are you going to do it?" Tori asked back.

Skylar turned around and said, "Are you trying to pick a fight? I'm not interested."

"Grab a drink with me?" Tori asked, smiling at her.

"I have a team meeting," Skylar replied.

"I know. Me too. I was thinking after. Let's go to Calhoun's, like old times."

Skylar noticed Mia out of the corner of her eye. She was heading over to the dugout, which was behind where Skylar and Tori were standing.

"Mia, do you want to go to Calhoun's after the meeting? Maybe grab a few of the others?" she asked.

"I can't. I have to get Hazel from daycare," Mia replied, hefting her bat bag over her shoulder. Then, she looked at Tori. "You guys have fun, though."

"Okay. Jenny?" she asked as Jenny followed Mia inside to get her own bag.

"Maybe. I'll let you know. I have to check with the boyfriend."

"Whipped much?" Kai teased.

"Yes, and I have no problem with that."

"I meant just us, Sky," Tori whispered as she took a few steps closer to Skylar and placed a hand on her hip. "If you don't want to go, just say so. Don't invite your whole team just so you don't have to be alone with me."

Skylar looked down at the hand that she used to love in that position, and then turned to see Mia staring at the same gesture. There was hurt in Mia's eyes. Skylar could see that clear as day, which caused Skylar to think about that confusion Mia always seemed to bring about in her. Mia was a straight, single mother, who also happened to be her teammate. How was it that every time she looked over at Mia, it felt like something might be going unsaid between them?

"I'll meet you at Calhoun's when my meeting is over, okay?" she said.

"Yeah, okay." Tori removed her hand.

In the team meeting, there was a mild celebration for getting their first win. Then, they talked about the next game, which would take place the following afternoon. Jenny would start to give Mia's arm a rest, but Mia would come in if needed. They had Samford in reserve if both of them needed help, but Skylar was starting to think Mia's arm was bionic.

"I'll see you tomorrow," Skylar said as she and Mia walked to their cars after the meeting.

"Have fun tonight," Mia replied.

"It's not a big deal. Tori probably just wants to rehash the break-up – which I'm not interested in, but I kind of feel like I owe her." She shrugged.

"Closure. It's different for everyone. For my ex, it involved a messy divorce and signing over his paternal rights."

"What?" Sky asked as she hit the button to unlock her car. "He just—"

"Signed over his daughter, yeah," Mia interrupted. "The worst part was that he used her as a bargaining chip first. He was so angry with me, he threatened to take her away, when he never wanted kids to begin with. When I told him I was moving here, we had the first real conversation we'd had in a long time, and I convinced him it would be easier if he just terminated his rights."

"That's petty." Sky tossed her bat bag into the backseat of her car. "Did you even do anything to make him that angry, or was it just his fragile male ego?"

"Oddly enough, it was both." Mia laughed a little and shifted the bat bag on her shoulders. "He thought I was cheating – which I wasn't. He was, though, and had been for a while, but that's another story. The part that seemed to get to him was an unadvised confession I gave, which I probably shouldn't have."

"You said you weren't cheating… What was the confession?"

Mia looked around at the other players who weren't paying any attention to them, but who were still walking through the parking lot, so Mia took a few steps closer to her.

"I had feelings for someone that wasn't my husband. I didn't *do* anything, but I had fallen in love with someone else. I made the mistake of telling him that. I don't know. I guess I thought we could talk through it, go to counseling or something. But he took it hard, and we never recovered."

"That sucks," Skylar said because she didn't know what else to say.

"I think what really got to him was who I was having feelings for."

"Was it his brother or something?" Skylar tried to lighten the mood.

"No, it was a woman."

***

"Do you still not drink when you're playing?" Tori asked.

"No," Skylar replied.

"Well, I'm having a glass of wine," Tori replied, leaned over the bar, and ordered a red before she returned her attention to Skylar, who was staring at the door of the bar. "Sky?"

"Yeah?"

"Where are you right now?"

"What?"

"You're not here. I know that look. You're somewhere else. Why did you come out with me?"

"I thought you wanted to talk," she answered honestly.

"I did, but you obviously don't." Tori grabbed the wine that was placed on the bar in front of her. "Do you want a water or something?"

"No, I'm okay."

"Sky, I miss you." She placed her free hand on Skylar's knee.

"Tori, we—"

"I know. We broke up, but I can't help how I feel."

"I loved you, Tor. A part of me will always love you, but I'm not *in* love with you anymore. You deserve someone who is."

"You know what I miss most?" the woman asked as she sipped on her wine.

"Tor—"

"Do you remember what you used to do for me before games and before finals I was worried about?"

"Come on, Tori. This isn't productive."

Skylar did remember what Tori was talking about. She couldn't not. Tori got nervous before major tests and big games, and Skylar always found time to make sure Tori was properly relaxed. It usually began with a shoulder massage and then evolved into Skylar's head between Tori's legs.

"That's what I miss the most." Tori's hand slid up Skylar's thigh. "Are you doing that with someone else yet? Mia Landis, maybe?"

"What? No."

Mia… Skylar had been thinking about the bomb Mia had dropped the entire drive over. She'd wanted to ask so many questions, but Tom had approached with his family, wanting them to meet his players. Mia had left immediately after to pick up Hazel, leaving Skylar to stand there with her jaw open. Mia was attracted to women. She was at least attracted to one woman, which made it possible, in Skylar's opinion, that Mia was attracted or could be attracted to another woman; Skylar herself, maybe.

"You like her, though." Tori kept her hand in place.

"Tori, stop. Come on."

"I don't think you want me to stop. I know you, Sky. You're interested in her. You're stopping yourself from pursuing anything because she's on the team and maybe some other reason I don't know about, but that means you're probably pretty hard up right now, and I am also pretty hard up right now because my ex-girlfriend is sexy as hell, and I can't stop remembering all the times we–"

"We aren't doing anything, Tori."

"You and me, or you and Mia?" she asked, hovering her hand over Skylar's sex in plain view of the bar. "If you want me to stop, just pull my hand away."

Skylar did just that. Then, she stood.

"I thought you wanted to talk."

"I do. I want to talk about us."

"That's not talking. That's something else entirely."

"We can do both. Sky, I promise it doesn't have to mean anything. I get that you're done with this, but I miss you. I thought we could *reconnect*."

"If you still love me, how can you say it wouldn't mean anything?"

"Because I need it, Sky." Tori stood up, too. "There was this woman in Boise. We went on a date, and I went back to her place after, and it was nothing like how it is with you and me. I don't know that I'll have that again."

"You're twenty-two, Tori. It just feels like that now, but I'm not the one you're supposed to be with."

"Does it bother you that I was with someone else?" Tori asked.

"Not how you probably hope it does." Skylar placed a hand on Tori's cheek. "Tori, you will always be special to me. I want you to be so happy." She smiled at her. "If it's not that woman, there will be another, and you'll look back at me and think about how wrong you were that we ever even dated." She chuckled, trying to lighten the mood. "I should go."

"Do you really like her? I'm not teasing or trying to

give you a hard time. I just know you really well, Sky. You used to look at me like that."

Skylar dropped her hand from Tori's cheek and said, "I don't know."

"I think maybe you do. You just don't want to deal with it."

CHAPTER 15

IT WASN'T a big deal. Mia had just come out to a teammate that she had a major crush on. That crush happened to be a sexy lesbian, with a sexy and young ex. God, Tori was young. According to the league's website, Victoria Ray was twenty-two years old. Mia had tried not to think about how Skylar had spent the evening and maybe more with Tori during the three-game weekend. The Boomers had won two out of the three, and both of the games that Mia had pitched. Jenny and Samford had pitched the third game since Cheryl wanted to save Mia's arm. Mia felt good. She didn't need rest, but Cheryl pointed out that Mia was playing in the upcoming NORCECA event and that she'd need to keep her arm ready to go.

Mia and Skylar had both been called up, which was amazing, but it also gave them more time together, and things had been somewhat awkward since Mia had told her about being attracted to women. She expected a lot of questions once they had some alone time together, but surprisingly, Skylar hadn't asked her anything about it. They had practiced with the national team a few times, which felt like old times to Mia, but she could sense that Skylar was in awe of the whole thing. This was the first step for her. She'd been a coach before, but there was nothing like representing her country as a player, especially for someone like Skylar.

"Hey, how's the wrist?" Mia asked when they arrived at the hotel.

"It's fine. It's a little sore, honestly. I accidentally left my brace at home."

"Sky, you're supposed to wear it while you're healing whenever you're not playing," Mia scolded.

"The PT will wrap it for me. It's only aching because I've been lugging my bat bag and my carry-on around all day."

"Well, here," Mia said, quickly taking the handle of Skylar's bag and then moving to lift her bat bag off her shoulder and placing it over her own. "Now, go talk to the trainers about getting it wrapped before bed."

"Yes, ma'am." Skylar gave her a mock-salute.

"I'll get the room keys and meet you by the elevators."

"Okay, Number One." She smiled and headed in the direction of the coaching staff sitting in the lobby.

The event was in Toronto over the next five days. There were eight countries vying for the first-ever championship. The US would play the Dominican Republic first, and then, the winner of Canada and Mexico if they won that. It would be a long few days with little sleep since they'd be watching game film when they weren't playing, or they'd be in meetings or practice. Mia had the babysitter watching Hazel again. She hated leaving her daughter for long stretches, but she convinced herself that it was for the best.

"Checking in. Landis and Donahue." She passed her ID to the front desk agent. "I'm Landis. Donahue is over there, but can I just check us in?"

"Sure." The front desk clerk took a quick look at her ID. "You're already registered with the team, so you just need your room key."

"I'll take hers, too."

"No problem."

The woman passed Mia both keys, and Mia headed to the elevator with her stuff as well as Skylar's. She watched as the trainer wrapped Skylar's wrist up for the night, and only then did the nervousness really kick in. She and Skylar would be sharing a hotel room for the next four nights. She swallowed hard at the thought of being in a confined space with the woman. Mia hadn't ever been in a hotel room like this with someone she had a crush on. That was what this was. It was a crush. Well, it was a crush that had already provided her with many, many orgasms. She just wouldn't be able to have any of those this week.

"You ready?" Skylar asked.

"Are you?" Mia asked back.

"Because we're playing Chicago? The team is playing without us right now. Are you sending Cheryl your notes or something?" Mia asked.

"Notes, yes. To Cheryl, no. I'm sending them to Megan, actually." Skylar pulled out her laptop and placed it on the bed.

"Megan? Why?" Mia sat on the side of the bed.

"Because I'm scouting for her. That's my part-time job and why I didn't need the Little League one you got or any of the other coaching gigs." She pulled out her toiletry bag. "I spoke very highly of you, by the way."

"You scouted me?" Mia asked, not knowing if she was happy or upset about that.

"They already knew about you, obviously. All I did was tell them how amazing you still are as a player. Megan asked me to be a scout for the US team while I'm playing in the league since I know the US team well and will know the players and teams in the league well, too. It made sense."

"And does anyone on the team know?" Mia asked.

"Just you." Skylar sat down across from her on the other bed. "I haven't been keeping it a secret or anything, but I don't think I want it getting out there, though." She stared at Mia for a moment. "I trust you, Mia."

"Thanks."

"I guess I think that if everyone knew, they'd try to get me to pitch them to this team, and there are only twenty-two spots on this team. There are eight teams in that league with twenty-three players each, and the national team is already pretty stacked. The only reason I'm here is because a catcher is rehabbing an injury. I don't even know if I'd make the regular roster otherwise, and she's coming back, so this might be the only chance I get to wear red, white, and blue."

"So, you didn't scout yourself?" Mia teased, trying to take the worry away from Skylar.

Skylar smiled then and said, "No, I didn't. If I had still been a pitcher, they wouldn't have called me up. You would be getting the shot."

"In a way, your injury helped you out, huh?"

"I suppose it did." Sky chuckled. "Anyway, can you maybe help me wrap this thing up so that I can shower? I have some sports tape in my bag, and there's probably an extra trash bag inside that trash can. I just don't want to have to find PT to have them re-wrap it." She held up her arm.

"No problem. Find the tape. I'll get the bag."

***

After they'd both showered, Mia looked over at Skylar, who was watching game film on her bed. She had her headphones in, so Mia thought she wouldn't disturb her if she called to check on Hazel.

"Hello," the babysitter greeted.

"Hi, it's Mia. Is Hazel asleep already?"

"She just went down, actually."

"Oh," Mia replied, disappointed. "I guess that's a good thing, right?"

"Yes, I'd say so." The babysitter laughed.

"Is she okay?"

"She's fine. She's fine. She played with the two other girls I babysit for during the day at the park for a couple of hours. They mostly played with blocks on the blanket, but she had fun. I took a short video. I can send it to you. I just haven't had the time."

"That would be great. Thank you so much."

"Would you like me to keep her up a little later tomorrow night so you can say goodnight to her?"

115

"I should be in earlier tomorrow. Our flight got delayed, and there was a long line at customs. Then, I had to settle in, and I lost track of time. I should have called sooner."

"Forgive yourself, Mia. You're trying to make a life for your child."

"I know. I can't help feeling guilty for being away from her, though."

"How about I message you tomorrow night before I put her down?"

"That would be perfect. Thank you so much."

"Not a problem."

Mia disconnected the call, feeling tears welling up in her eyes. She sniffled and wiped the tear that fell.

"Are you okay?" Skylar asked softly.

"What?" Mia turned to see Skylar staring at her. "I'm fine. Sorry. I–"

"You don't have to pretend you don't miss your daughter, Mia." Skylar placed her laptop on the bed, moved over to Mia's, and sat beside her.

"I was hoping to say goodnight to her, but she's already asleep." Mia wiped another tear.

"Can you call her in the morning before practice?"

"Yeah, but… I don't know. I just hate not saying goodnight to her."

"Can I do anything? We can watch a movie or something; take your mind off it or–"

"No, I'm okay. You can go to sleep. I know you're tired. I'm just having a moment." Mia's phone beeped. "She sent the video."

"Who did?"

"The babysitter. She's amazing. I really lucked out finding her. She took a video of Hazel playing earlier." Mia clicked on the message. "Do you want to watch it with me?"

"Sure." Skylar scooted closer to her.

Mia pressed play, and the video of her little girl stacking alphabet blocks on top of a Paw Patrol blanket filled the phone screen. She turned it horizontally so that she could see it better.

"Hazel, can you say hi to your mama?" the babysitter asked from behind the camera.

Hazel looked over at the phone and said, "Hi, Mama."

Mia smiled and let another couple of tears fall as the video ended.

"She's beautiful," Skylar said, leaning into Mia's shoulder. "She looks just like you."

Mia avoided the second part of that and said, "Thank you."

"I realize I have no right to say this, because I'm not a parent and I'm not in your situation, but, Mia, you shouldn't feel guilty about being away from her when you're working to support her. Your ex-husband should be the one that feels guilty, but he really sounds like a shithead, so I doubt he feels much of anything. I don't know if this will make you feel any better, but I had two parents who never tucked me in or worried about saying goodnight to me."

"Really?" Mia turned her head to Skylar, who stretched her legs out on Mia's bed.

"Obviously, when I was in the crib, they had to put me to bed, but I'm pretty sure the moment I hit the toddler bed stage, they basically had my brothers put me to bed, or I did it myself."

"They made your brothers put you to bed?"

"My older brother, Sal Jr., was eight when I was born. Steven was six. We grew up in farm country, which meant they were both working from a pretty early age. I started waking up at five in the morning by the time I was five years old. I don't actually remember them putting me to bed or waking me up in the morning, either. They were already on the farm."

"Did it bother you?"

Skylar looked at her with a smirk and asked, "Are you asking me if they messed me up because they weren't around a lot?"

"I guess." Mia chuckled.

"If I'm messed up, it's not because of that." She winked. "All I'm saying is that parents have to do what they have to do. Had they put me to bed or woken me up in the morning, something on the farm wouldn't have been done. The farm was how we survived. I fault them for a lot of things, but I don't fault them for that. Hazel won't fault you for this, either. She'll understand when she's older, even if she can't now."

"Thank you, Sky."

"You don't have to thank me."

"Yes, I do." Mia sniffled again. "It's been really hard, and sometimes I feel like I'm barely hanging in there."

"I'm here. If you need to talk, I'm here."

CHAPTER 16

"CAN you tell me what it was like?"

"Coming out?" Skylar asked the following night after they'd returned to the room following the team dinner.

"Yes."

"Are you thinking about doing that yourself or…"

"I'm sorry. I shouldn't have just brought it up like that. We were going to talk about the game tomorrow. I think the one through three hitters are on top of fastballs. How about we try some knuckleballs and curves and see how that goes in the first inning?"

Skylar lay on her bed after grabbing the wrist brace the physical therapist had procured for her, and put it on.

"Mia, I didn't exactly come out."

"What does that mean?"

"It means there was a barn dance in my tiny town. Yes, that's a thing." She paused and watched Mia smile. "At this barn dance, there was this girl. Her name was Alice. She was a year older, and I knew that she was like me. Well, I knew she'd slept with a friend of a friend who had gone off to community college and left her behind. Anyway, that friend of a friend was a girl, so I knew she was at least interested; even if it was an experiment for her, I wanted her. I'd never even kissed a girl, but I knew in my bones that that was what I was supposed to do. We'd been talking, passing notes and whatnot." She smiled at the memory. "And, that night, I went to the dance with a boy I had absolutely no interest in. She did the same with another boy. We ditched them and met outside. We took a walk, and after talking for a while, we kissed. It was sloppy and all over the place at first, but then we found our rhythm, and it was nice. I'd kissed a girl, and I definitely liked it. I wanted more. So did she. So we kind of got hot and heavy, and hands were moving places. Lips were on skin. It was pretty fast, and I don't even remember the moment her hand slid up under the skirt I'd been forced to wear by my mother. Right before she could move any further, though, someone coughed. Another person laughed, and the boys we'd brought as dates realized they'd been duped."

"Oh, no."

"The rumors started right after. Alice never talked to me again. That's my coming out story."

"That's terrible. I'm sorry, Sky."

"Me too." She sighed.

"What about your parents?"

"They are pretty religious, so being gay isn't something they're big fans of. They don't like to talk about it, and they don't want to know about it, so we kind of just pretend like I have no personal life."

"That sucks."

"I'm used to it by now, but I do wish I could share that part of my life with them. When I was with Tori, I tried to talk to my mom about her once. She changed the subject to the weather. I tried again a little later, and then she asked if I'd been to church recently. I gave up after that."

Mia rolled onto her side to face Skylar. They were on their separate beds. Mia had her shoulder wrapped in ice. They'd won the first two games of the tournament, but Skylar's wrist had caused some problems. There was an errant throw to second as a player attempted to steal that ended up in center field and cost them a run. Then, there was a passed ball that Skylar should have been able to stop, but she'd had to place her hand on the ground to stop herself from falling and felt the pain shoot through her hand and up her arm to her shoulder. Those had not been her best moments, but they'd won, and Mia had pitched well.

They now had the championship game left that they would play against Puerto Rico. Skylar would be catching for the whole game. Mia would likely come in as the reliever if needed since they weren't too worried about Puerto Rico. Mia had impressed Megan and the coaching staff enough. She'd make the team for the next tournament, at least, without a problem.

"Did you think Tori was the one?" she asked.

"I guess everyone thinks that at some point during a serious relationship, right? If not, what's the point?"

"What changed?"

"When do *I* get to ask you a bunch of deeply personal questions?" she teased and rolled onto her side to face Mia.

"I guess that's fair." Mia smiled. "Shoot."

"What made you fall for your ex?"

"Gregg?" she asked as if Skylar would know about any others. "We met in college. He was a soccer star. I was a softball star. Match made in heaven, right?"

"That doesn't actually answer my question."

"He was sweet back then. We both put sports ahead of pretty much everything else. We wanted the same things, and it worked."

"Then, he cheated?"

"Then, he kept thinking he deserved more in soccer when he was putting in less. He got mad when he got dropped from a team, and that's when the cheating started, I think. He didn't like that I was still playing the sport I loved when he couldn't. I tried to make things work, but–" Mia stopped.

"But, what?"

"But that's when I told him about Francesca, the woman I fell for."

"And his ego got in the way of his acceptance?"

"I think me having feelings for anyone else would have been an issue, obviously, but me telling him I was thinking about being with another woman just made it worse. Unfortunately, then I got pregnant. Don't get me wrong; I don't regret it. My daughter is the best thing in my life, and I'm glad it happened. But the timing was pretty bad. On top of that, Gregg had never wanted kids, and I was living my dream on the national team, so I wasn't prepared for pregnancy or what that would mean. At first, I thought I could come back to the team after, but then the divorce was so messy, I couldn't put the effort the team would deserve into playing."

"I get that."

"That's the story." Mia sighed.

"Can I ask about *her*?"

"Francesca?"

"Yes." Skylar chuckled.

"She was amazing." Mia smiled. "When Gregg and I started the separation and divorce proceedings, I thought she and I would have a shot, but that didn't happen."

"Why not?"

"She was worried that I was just coming out of a relationship, and she thought I needed some time on my own. Plus, she had just started dating someone. She'd had no idea I was about to leave my husband and ask her to be more than just a friend."

"So, I take it, she wasn't in love with you?"

"I thought she was. But she was gay and out. I guess she was more interested in a woman who was one hundred percent ready to be with her with little to no baggage." Mia paused. "The kid thing was also an issue."

"She didn't want them?"

"She did, but she wanted kids with her future wife, not with a future wife and that wife's ex-husband. It just didn't work out."

"Can I ask another question?" Skylar picked at a rogue thread on the brace that was a little too tight for her wrist, considering it was slightly swollen.

"Yes."

"Are you…"

"Gay?"

"Yeah, I just couldn't find a good way to ask it. You'd think I'd be better at that by now." She laughed lightly at herself.

"I'm bisexual. That's the best label I can come up with, at least. I never knew until I met Francesca that I was into women. When I met her, it was just completely clear that I could also fall in love with and be with a woman."

"And you weren't ever with her?"

"No."

Skylar licked her lips before she asked, "Have you ever—"

"Yes." Mia licked her own lips, which caused Skylar to lower her eyes to them and consider what it would feel like to drag her tongue along them or to have Mia's tongue on her own, doing the same. "Twice."

"Same woman?"

"Two different women."

"And?"

"And, what?" Mia laughed and rolled over onto her back.

"How was it?"

"Which time?"

"Both times." Skylar laughed, too.

"Bad, and then good."

"Yeah?"

"The first woman and I just didn't have any chemistry. The second woman and I definitely had chemistry, but only in the bedroom."

"Really? That good?"

"Mind-blowing," Mia said. "Best orgasm of my life."

"Only one?"

"Huh?" Mia turned her head to Skylar and stared at her inquisitively.

Skylar smirked and asked, "Did she only give you one?"

"Oh." Mia appeared to think about that. "Yes. I guess, yeah."

"That's a shame." Skylar rolled onto her back and smirked toward the ceiling.

"Really?" Mia laughed.

"I can't say I've ever left a woman after giving her only one, but maybe your girl wasn't much of a giver."

"Hey." Mia laughed louder at that.

"Men aren't great with multiples either, obviously, unless they're willing to be givers or take a while in between."

"Why are we even talking about this?" Mia laughed through her question.

"Because I'm wondering if you've ever had truly mind-blowing sex before, Mia."

"I just told—"

Skylar sat up quickly, hung her feet over the side of the bed, stared at Mia, and said, "I'm talking about toe-curling; fingers gripping the sheets with white knuckles, sweat covering your skin and their skin because you've been going at it for hours. You can't keep your hands from their skin, and they can't keep theirs from yours, so they just keep touching and stroking and licking and sucking and kissing until you come again and again. And, eventually, you lie there completely sated, thinking you'll never need another orgasm again, but then, they reach over and touch you, because they can't not, and it's like you can't live without it again all of a sudden." She swallowed. "Have you ever had that kind of mind-blowing, earth-shattering sex, Mia?"

"Have you?" Mia asked back, staring at Skylar's lips.

Had Skylar had sex like that? She'd thought so. She'd been with a few women where the sex was amazing. There had definitely been multiple orgasms. She had been up all night, touching them, and vice versa. Sex with Tori had been even better because they had been in love. It had meant more with Tori than the others, but as she stared at Mia Landis, Skylar wondered about the question. Mia's hand moved to her own hip. She was wearing a pair of gray sweats she'd cut into shorts. Her legs were long, bare, and glistened in their smoothness. Her black tank top left little to the imagination. Skylar wasn't so sure anymore that she'd had that mind-blowing, earth-shattering sex. She wished she could have some right now, with the woman lying in the other bed, but Mia Landis was off-limits for more reasons than one.

"Wouldn't you like to know?" she teased.

Mia just rolled her eyes in response.

CHAPTER 17

"MIA, is she okay?" Megan asked.

"Skylar?"

"Yes, she's stiff back there." Megan pointed at Skylar, who was behind the plate, catching warm-up pitches before the start of the third inning.

"It's probably just because it's the warm-up," she lied.

"No, she's been like this the whole game." Megan gave an exasperated sigh. "If she misses another throw to second, or another ball gets passed her, I have to take her out." She looked over at Mia, who didn't say anything. "How's your arm?"

"Fine."

"Let's see how this inning goes. If I need you to go in, are you ready?"

"Yeah, no problem."

Megan nodded. Then, she turned her attention to the field. When the inning started, they were up by two runs, but by the time they'd gotten one out, the game was tied. There was a runner on second, and the batter had two balls and no strikes. On the next pitch, the batter moved to bunt. She barely tapped the ball forward. Skylar quickly removed her mask, tossing it aside, and picked up the ball. Instead of throwing it to first for the out, though, she caught sight of the runner heading to third. She threw the ball in the direction of the shortstop who was covering third, but the ball went over her head and into the outfield. Now, they were down by one, with a runner on second base and only one out.

"Time," Megan called. "Grab your glove."

Mia did. Then, she followed Megan to the mound. Mia had already warmed up, so she felt loose and ready to go. Skylar went to the mound with her head down. When Mia moved toward her, Skylar tucked her glove under her shoulder and massaged her hand.

"Are you okay?"

"It hurts a little," Skylar said.

"Sky, do you need to come out?" Megan asked her.

"It's a little achy, but I'm okay. That ball just got away from me. It hit the dirt and got covered in the stuff. It was slippery."

"Mia's coming in. Let's bring this home, ladies." Megan took the ball from the other pitcher and put it into Mia's glove. "Sky, tell me now."

"I'm good."

Megan nodded, but Mia knew that if something else happened, Skylar would be pulled out of the game.

"They can't hit my fastball. I'll hit the targets, okay? You shouldn't have to throw anyone else out," Mia told her once they were alone.

"Yeah, okay."

Mia did hit her targets. The next inning, the US scored one run, tying it up. Mia struck out three batters in a row in the fourth inning. In the fifth, she struck out one, and there were two easy in-field hits the defense took care of. The US scored two runs that inning, and neither team scored again. The US won the first NORCECA Softball Championship. Skylar hadn't had any issues for the rest of the game, but Mia knew that her mistakes earlier on would weigh on her later.

The team had a celebratory dinner together. Then, they returned to their rooms to pack and get ready for their flights back home the following day. Mia showered first. Skylar had decided to go for a walk, likely needing some time alone. By the time she returned, Mia was on the phone.

"Hey, baby," she said to Hazel just as Skylar walked into the room. "How are you?"

"Mama," Hazel said in her adorable toddler voice.

"Sorry," Skylar whispered.

"It's okay," Mia whispered back. "She's two. It won't be a long conversation."

Mia returned her attention to the phone, but then she caught sight of Skylar pulling off her t-shirt and tossing it on the bed. She had seen the woman in a sports bra many times, but seeing her half-dressed in a hotel room allowed Mia's mind to wander. Skylar kicked off her sweats, and without a word, she moved into the bathroom and turned on the shower. She seemed unhappy about something. Mia was sure it was how she'd played, but she didn't want to broach the subject unless Skylar brought it up.

"Goodnight, sweet girl," she said just as Skylar exited the bathroom fully dressed for sleep.

"Night, Mama," Hazel replied.

Then, before Mia could ask her to hand the phone back to her babysitter, Hazel had managed to hang up on her. Mia laughed.

"Something funny?" Skylar asked, sliding into her bed.

"She hung up on me."

"Hazel?"

"Yeah."

"She's two."

"Well, I guess she's old enough to know the bright red button means hang up on her mother."

"Listen, I'm sorry about today," Skylar said.

"What do you mean?"

"I didn't play well. I let the team down."

"Sky, we won."

"I should have taken myself out in the second inning when the pain got bad."

"Hey, everyone has a bad inning. You recovered fine." Mia rolled onto her side to face her.

"I was worried that this was my only shot, and I think I ruined it."

"It was one game, Sky."

"Megan told me she's not calling me up for the Worlds."

"What?"

"Don't worry. You're on the team, Number One. She's sending me back to the minor leagues, so to speak. She said my wrist needs more time to heal. I know she felt bad about it, but it still sucks."

"Sky, I'm so sorry."

"The other catcher will be back by then. I should have guessed. I just hoped I would be good enough." Skylar stared up at the ceiling. "I'm glad you played well, though."

"Do you want to talk about it?"

"No, I think I just want to get some sleep," she said.

"Okay," Mia replied. "If you do, I'm here."

"Thanks." Skylar looked over at her, granting her the smallest of smiles.

***

"You can't do it?"

"No, Mia. I'm sorry."

The Women's Softball World Championship was rapidly approaching. The tournament itself had sixteen participants and represented a chance to qualify for the Olympics for the winner, well in advance of the next games. The event was held every two years. If they won this one, they were automatically qualified. If not, they'd have to wait another two years for the chance or win several additional tournaments to qualify. Of the sixteen teams, France, as the host nation, automatically qualified for the games, so they were up against fifteen other hopefuls.

Mia had been playing well with the Boomers as of late. When Megan called her to confirm what Sky had said that night about her being selected for the Worlds, she had been over the moon, but she had also been overwhelmed. She had games for the Boomers to play, games for the national team, and she also had a daughter that she wanted to spend time with, and who also needed someone to watch her whenever Mia wasn't around.

"It's fine. I understand. I'll call my mom and see if she can come to town for a couple of weeks," she said, disconnecting the call from the babysitter.

The tournament lasted over two weeks due to the travel and the games themselves. Her usual babysitter couldn't take her for that long, and Mia hated the idea of having Hazel bounce from one sitter to the other.

"Hi there."

"Hey, Mom."

"Everything okay?"

"How do you always know when things aren't okay when I literally say two words?"

"Because I'm your mother."

Mia laughed and said, "I'm running into a bit of a challenge."

"How can I help?"

"I need a sitter, and I can't find one that will take her for two weeks. I can't take her with me. The flight alone is long, and then I'll have a roommate, and the—"

"Hold on."

"Sorry."

"This is for that big tournament?"

"Yes."

"Well, I can be there. I can book a cheap flight and stay there with her."

"Really? You can?"

"Of course. I'm feeling a lot better. The doctor gave me permission to fly yesterday. I asked because I was planning to visit you. Maybe I can stay a few days after you get back to spend some time with you after I take care of my granddaughter."

"Mom, you're my hero. If I've never told you that, I'm

very, very sorry."

With that sorted, Mia could return her attention to the Boomers and their winning season. So far, they'd played every team, and they had beaten each one at least two out of three times, if not all three. They were at the top of the table and would undoubtedly at least be in the final championship game. Mia put her daughter to sleep and moved onto the sofa. It had been a while since she'd been able to find the time to treat herself to an orgasm. After helping Skylar with her stretching earlier that day during a shared workout, she needed to relieve the tension between her legs.

She turned on the TV, keeping the volume at just the right level. It never mattered what was on; she only needed it to drown out the sound. Hazel had been difficult to put down, for some reason, so Mia also grabbed one of the small pillows and placed it between her legs to help muffle the sound further. Then, she moved the vibrator between her legs, turned it on, and thought about what Skylar had said that night in the hotel room. She could hear it in Skylar's soft voice, almost word for word.

"I'm talking about toe-curling; fingers gripping the sheets with white knuckles, sweat covering your skin and their skin because you've been going at it for hours. You can't keep your hands from their skin, and they can't keep theirs from yours, so they just keep touching and stroking and licking and sucking and kissing until you come again and again. And, eventually, you lie there completely sated, thinking you'll never need another orgasm again, but then, they reach over and touch you, because they can't not, and it's like you can't live without it again all of a sudden. Have you ever had that kind of mind-blowing, earth-shattering sex, Mia?"

Mia came hard. She bit down on her lower lip to stop herself from screaming. When she was done, she whispered Skylar's name. Then, she gathered herself, slowed her breathing, and thought about the multiple orgasms Skylar had mentioned. She'd done that on her own before, but never with Gregg. He had been a one-and-done kind of guy and hadn't like oral sex. Well, he hadn't liked giving it. He'd never had a problem receiving it. So, as far as one orgasm right after another, both of them bleeding together in pleasure and ecstasy, she'd never done that with another person.

"What the hell?" she said to herself, started the vibrator up again, and let herself feel the ghost of Skylar's touch against her skin.

CHAPTER 18

"ARE you excited?" Skylar asked.

"I wish you were coming with me," Mia replied.

"Me too." She chuckled.

"Thank you for taking me to the airport. I just couldn't say goodbye to Hazel here, and my mom can't exactly just drop me off and leave her at the apartment."

"No problem. I'm happy to help." Skylar looked over at her. "I'll try to keep the team together while you're away. We have six games while you're gone. It's going to be tough with just Jenny and Samford."

"You need to be careful. It's just you and Kai behind the plate, and your wrist is—"

"Fine. I'm taking it easy. They've been wrapping it for games, and it seems to help. Plus, I'm going to PT again."

"That's good, Skylar."

Mia turned to the side when a knock hit the passenger window. It was a police officer giving them an incredulous look.

"You should hop out before I get a ticket for doing you a favor, Number One." Skylar smiled at her.

"I'll see you when I get back, okay?"

"You can call me, you know? While you're there. If you want." Skylar shrugged a shoulder. "If you just need someone to talk to or—"

"Okay. I will. It goes both ways, too."

"Okay," Skylar said.

Then, Mia climbed out of the car, gathered her bags

from the trunk, and disappeared into the crowd of people going into the airport. Skylar rejoined traffic and made her way to the doctor's office.

"Skylar, your x-rays are fine, so that's good," the doctor told her.

"Thank God. I sat out the last game. It about killed me."

"I still think we need an MRI. I want to make sure everything's really okay in there."

"Really?"

"Team's orders," she said. "When your coach called to make this appointment, she told me I was to give you the full workup and that I had to clear you to play."

"I know. She told me."

"I'm going to have you stop doing the exercises in PT until we get the results, but I still want you to go so that they can massage it. I'll write up the order for the MRI. Make the appointment as soon as you can."

"I will. I want to play," she replied.

An hour later, she'd hung up from the MRI clinic. They didn't have an available appointment for two weeks. She hated hearing that news, so she called another clinic about thirty miles away in the same network. They had an appointment available, but not until the following week. There were two more clinics on the list. Skylar called one forty miles away with no luck. The one that was over an hour away had an appointment for the day after next. She locked that in, feeling a bit better about her luck, and reached for her laptop.

She had some scouting to do for the national team. Despite the fact that she hadn't made it on the team that went to this tournament, she still had a chance of getting called up again if she could just sort out her damn injury. Megan would never settle for only having her existing roster. She would always be looking for the next round of talent. So, Skylar watched some game film, studying the players one by one. She started with the seven other teams in the league, writing up her recommendations to send to Megan later, but then she moved onto college players. By the time she'd made it through game film for over twelve promising players, it was time for her to get her MRI results.

"Hey," Skylar greeted Mia.

"Hi. Is now an okay time?" Mia asked.

Skylar moved the phone to her other hand and said, "Can I call you back in, like, twenty or thirty minutes? I'm at a PT appointment," she lied.

"Oh, sure. Sorry. I should have texted first. I just had some time, but we're headed back to the hotel now, so call me whenever."

"Okay," she said, hating to have to hang up on Mia for their very first call after the woman had gone away.

They disconnected just as the doctor walked in and sat down on the rolling stool in front of her.

"Well, the good news is that from what I can tell, you don't need another surgery."

"That *is* good news." Skylar let out a deep sigh of relief.

"The bad news is that you need rest, Skylar." The doctor sighed this time. "I'm prescribing two weeks of absolutely no softball; PT massages every other day, at a minimum, and that you wear that brace at all times unless you have it wrapped up properly."

"I can't do that. I have games to play," she said.

"Skylar, if you want to survive to play another season, you have to rest your hand. You have to give the soft tissue the time it needs to heal."

"What about an injection?"

"Those don't fix the problem. They hide it."

"But, it could get me through the rest of the season. Then, I can rest it in the off-season, right?"

"You're still out for at least the next week, Sky. Your hand will swell due to the injection. It's going to hurt."

"I still want to do it."

"I'll make you a deal."

"Okay. Whatever it is, okay."

The doctor smiled and said, "I'll give you the shot today, you go to daily PT massages, and you don't play or practice until I see the wrist in a week. One week instead of two; that's the best I can do. If I don't like how it looks in a week, you're taking another two off."

"You drive a hard bargain," Skylar said, squinting at the doctor.

"I'll get the paperwork for the injection. But, Skylar, this is the only one. After that, you're letting this heal the right way, no matter what's going on in softball."

***

"How does it feel to be one game away from being a world champion?" Skylar asked as she lay on her sofa, talking to Mia on the phone.

"It'll feel better when we actually win and are guaranteed a spot in the games," Mia replied.

"I bet."

"Sky, I talked to Megan about you. I hope that's okay."

"You did?" she asked.

Skylar had had a rough week and a half. The injection had only just started to help with the pain. She had gotten the massages every day and had stayed on the anti-inflammatories the doctor had recommended. She'd also missed all of the games the Boomers had played in order to rest it properly. She was growing restless. She couldn't practice, so she just had to sit in the dugout or walk around the field. She couldn't play in the games, so she had to live vicariously through Kai, and the team that she had wanted to be on her entire life was on ESPN, vying for a world championship without her. It broke her heart in a way, but it had also made her smile. Mia had pitched in three of the games and was on tap for the championship start. She had played well, and Skylar loved watching that woman hurl a fastball toward an unsuspecting batter.

"I did. I told her that you were resting your hand, like the doctor told you, and that you'd had the MRI, and you didn't need surgery. She seemed happy about that."

"It doesn't matter. I ruined my shot."

"No, you didn't. She knows what you know. She's got two great catchers on the roster, but one of them is about to retire, and the other wants to have a kid soon. Paris – at least as far as I can tell – is up for grabs for catchers. You rest now and get your wrist back in good working order, Sky, and you could be in the Olympics."

"With you?" she asked, smiling at the thought.

"I guess. I mean, it's a few years away, and anything can happen. Hazel comes first, so–"

"Just dream with me for a minute, Mia," she requested. "Picture it. It's 2024. We're both dressed in the red, white, and blue. We're marching in those opening ceremonies, waving the tiny flags, and then we're playing that first game. You're pitching. I'm catching. You throw a no-hitter."

"Not a perfect game?" Mia asked, chuckling; and, God, Skylar liked that.

"Not yet. Be patient," she said.

"Okay." Mia's laughter continued.

"We make it to the gold medal game. It's you on the mound and me behind the plate again. That's where you throw the perfect game; the first-ever, as far as I know, and we win. I throw the mask off and rush to the mound to–" She stopped.

"To what?" Mia asked.

Skylar knew what she'd been about to say, but she couldn't really say it; not now, and probably not ever.

"Hug you," she replied.

Mia didn't say anything for a long moment.

"Right," she finally let out. "A hug."

"And then, the dogpile would start. Everyone would jump all over each other, and we'd do the Gatorade dump on Megan."

"Hey, Sky?"

Oh, shit… Skylar had gotten herself into this mess. She'd have to lie her way out of it.

"Yeah?"

"Oh, hold on." Mia paused. "That's my mom calling. Can I call you back?"

"No problem."

"Okay. Thanks."

Saved by the phone call. Skylar placed the phone on her chest and stared up at the ceiling of her apartment. Her heart was racing. She'd wanted to kiss Mia. She'd pictured them winning the game and rushing to her to capture her lips in an all-consuming kiss. She wanted a moment just like Wyatt Wicked had had with the woman she'd been thinking about since the moment she'd laid eyes on her. Her phone rang again after only a minute or so. She smiled as she picked it up.

"That was fast."

"Sky, my mom was taken to the hospital."

"What?" Skylar shot up off the sofa.

"She called me. They're just running some tests, and they're saying she's fine, but it's her back. She must have thrown it out picking up Hazel or something."

"What can I do?" she asked.

"Hazel is at the hospital with her. They'll release my mom tomorrow morning probably, but she can't take care of Hazel tonight and shouldn't do it tomorrow. I'm going to book a flight right now, but I was wondering if you could go to the hospital and pick up Hazel for me. I know it's a lot to ask. I'm going to call her usual sitter to see if she can take her for the night, and I'll be back as soon as I can tomorrow."

"I can watch her," she blurted out. "I'll pick her up, check on your mom, and bring Hazel back here. I can watch her."

"I can't ask that of you."

"Yes, you can. I'm not doing anything anyway. Let me watch her, Mia."

"Are you sure?"

"Yeah. I'll need a car seat for my car, though, right?" she asked, remembering Mia's comment from before.

"They took my mom in an ambulance. My car is at my place."

"I'll drive over and pick it up."

"There's a key under the front mat. I left it there just in case I needed the babysitter to stop by. That'll get you into the apartment. I'm sure she left the car keys on the counter or something."

"I'll find them. I'll leave right now."

"Sky, thank you. I'm looking up flights on my computer now."

"Hazel will be fine. I'll call you when I'm home with her, and I'll make sure your mom has what she needs. You can focus on the game tomorrow."

"I should leave now. I just don't know if—"

"The flight is hours long, Mia. Just stay. The game is at eight in the morning. Leave right after, if you have to, but I promise you, I will take care of her. I can take care of her and make sure your mom is okay."

"I'll send you my flight information as soon as I have something booked."

"Okay. I'll call you as soon as I can, okay?"

"Sky, this is beyond teammate. It's beyond friend, even. It's—"

"Mia?"

"Yeah?"

"When you get back, we'll talk, okay? Right now, don't worry about your family. Just win one more game and come home. Okay?"

"Yeah, okay."

CHAPTER 19

MIA had just won the World Championship. She had a trophy and a medal to prove it, but the moment the game was over, she'd tucked the medal into her bat bag and rushed to a waiting car. Megan and the rest of the team had been very supportive and understanding. They'd arranged for the car and her flight home to allow her to get there as quickly as possible. Skylar had also checked in numerous times. She'd picked Hazel up at the hospital in Mia's car. She had also stayed at the hospital for a bit with Mia's mom, getting her some non-hospital food and whatever update she could so that she could get it to Mia. According to the doctors, Mia's mom had slipped a disc and had broken a bone in her wrist and a rib on the way down in the fall. It was painful, but nothing serious, and she wouldn't have to remain in the hospital beyond today. They were only keeping her as long because of her previous fall and injuries.

The flight home was unbearably long. Mia couldn't sleep. She couldn't focus on the book she tried to read or the movie she tried to watch. She could only think about both her daughter and her mother needing her, and her being too far away to help. Then, she thought of Skylar, and she smiled as she sipped on her ginger ale. Skylar had dropped everything to rush to take care of Mia's family. She had sent Mia pictures and even a video where she'd coached Hazel to say that she was okay and that her mommy should win her game. It was adorable. Mia had already saved it to her phone and played it over and over. When she arrived at the airport, she looked for the car the team had arranged. Instead, she saw Skylar standing at baggage claim, holding Hazel against her hip.

"Oh, my God!" Mia rushed toward them.

"Hey. I thought we'd come get you," Skylar said.

"You are amazing!" Mia took Hazel into her arms and held her close. "Hi, baby."

"Hi, Mama." Hazel's chubby arms went around her neck.

"How are you?"

"Sky is funny," she replied.

"She is?" Mia asked, looking over at Skylar, who was looking back at her.

Skylar still had her hand on the small of Hazel's back as if she hadn't wanted to let her go. The whole scene was oddly intimate. To anyone looking at them, it would appear that they were a couple. Mia had been away, and now she was home, and her family was picking her up at the airport. She smiled at that thought.

"I am very funny. You didn't know that about me?" Skylar teased.

"You are the best person," Mia replied. "That I *do* know."

"It was nothing. She's a great kid, and your mom is doing well. She's getting released, actually. I thought I could take you to the hospital. We can pick her up, swing by a pharmacy if we need to, and then, I can take you home."

"Your car is at my place, isn't it?" Mia asked, hugging Hazel even closer.

"Yeah."

"I bet you can't wait to go back to your place without a toddler, huh?"

"I'm good." Skylar smiled genuinely at her. "I mean it. Hazel is cool. Right, Haze?"

"Sky." Hazel just said the name and then giggled.

"Haze?"

"Yeah, it's her cool new nickname. You're Number One. She's Haze." Skylar pressed the tip of her finger to Hazel's nose. "Right, little one?"

Hazel continued to giggle. Mia kissed her daughter's forehead, reached for Skylar's hand with her free one, and squeezed it.

"I will never be able to repay you for taking care of them for me."

Skylar squeezed it back and said, "You don't ever have to."

Then, the baggage claim buzzer sounded. Skylar held on to Mia's hand as they walked to the carousel, waiting for the bags. Mia couldn't help herself. With their hands linked, it was just so easy for her to rest her head on Skylar's shoulder. Skylar didn't move or protest, so she just left it there. When Skylar's fingers moved to intertwine with her own, Mia's heart started beating wildly.

"Can you take her for a second? I'll grab my bags. I don't want you to mess up your wrist," Mia said.

"Sure," Skylar replied, letting go of Mia's hand to take Hazel from her. "What do you think about worms?" she asked Hazel.

That caused Mia to turn back around to look at them.

"Gross," Hazel replied, shaking her head and scrunching her tiny nose at her.

"I like worms." Skylar tickled the toddler's tummy, earning a giggle. Then, she glanced up at Mia. "It's a game we've been playing."

"About worms?" Mia asked.

"Not worms, specifically. I ask what she thinks about something. She tells me it's gross. I tickle her. She laughs."

"Sky." Hazel laughed again after only saying Skylar's name.

"Yup." Mia tilted her head to the side to take in Skylar with her daughter. "Sky."

***

142

"Mom, are you okay?" Mia asked as she approached her mother's hospital bed.

"I'm fine. I'm fine. I'm just going to be moving a little slow for a while," she said, moving to shift uncomfortably in bed. "Are you here to pick me up? I have my paperwork ready."

"The doctor said it's okay for you to go? What's the aftercare look like?"

"He did. I have painkillers, and I have to use heat and ice for the disc, but my rib will heal on its own. I just have to take it easy. My wrist is in this cast for four weeks, though. Then, I get it off back home."

"Back home?" Mia asked. Then, she heard Hazel laughing from the hallway, which caused her to smile. "Mom, you're staying with me until you're all better."

"I like her," her mother replied, moving her head toward the open doorway.

"Who? What?"

"Skylar. I like her for you."

"Mom!" Mia whisper-yelled. "We're not together. She's a teammate."

"A teammate who practically ran to this hospital to check on me and *your* daughter. I understand team's bond, but that's a pretty big deal, Mia. She took Hazel to her house and took care of her for us so we wouldn't worry. She even stayed a bit with me to make sure I was okay."

"I know. She's pretty great."

"So, nothing? Really?" her mother teased.

Mia glared at her and whispered, "I like her."

"So, I was right."

"No, nothing's happened. And it can't, Mom. We're on the same team. We're both trying to make the Olympic roster. It's complicated."

"I read an article about two women who played in the Olympics together. They were a couple."

"What?" Mia chuckled. "You did?"

"When you first told me about liking women, I did

some research. I wanted to understand. There was an article about two professional soccer players. They play on the same team, and they played in the Olympics together; World Cup, too. If they can do it, why can't you two?"

"We just met, Mom."

"Oh, it's been months at this point." The older woman waved her off with the hand that wasn't in a cast. "Anyway, we can talk more about that later. Let's get Hazel home. Oh, and I'm not staying with you for four weeks, Mia. That apartment is barely big enough for the two of you. With me there, it's even more crowded. I'll stay for a couple of days, just until I'm okay to fly. And then, I'll head home."

"Mom, it's—"

"Mia, I have people back home who can take care of me. I won't be alone. Besides, you'll be traveling with the team on some days. It's better for me to be at home. My doctors are there, too."

"Are you sure?"

"I'm sure I'm ready to get out of this place."

***

"Thank you," Mia said for the millionth time.

"You don't have to keep thanking me," Skylar told her.

They were in the parking lot of Mia's complex, standing next to Skylar's car. Hazel was asleep in her bed; Mia's mom was asleep in Mia's. Mia would be taking the sofa for the next few nights.

"I'm buying you dinner; many dinners, I think," she said.

Skylar smiled and replied, "I'm down for that."

"My mom will be here for a few days. After that, we can hit that restaurant on the way to the field; the one with–"

"Hey, Mia?" Skylar interrupted.

Mia swallowed and said, "Yeah?"

Skylar took a step toward her, leaving little space between them, and said, "You're beautiful." Then, she placed a hand on Mia's cheek, and the other one, wrapped up in tape, on her hip. "Like really, really beautiful."

"So are you," Mia said without thinking.

Skylar's smile was also beautiful. Mia looked down at the woman's lips. Then, her eyes flitted up to Skylar's, which were darker now. Skylar's hand on her cheek slid back behind Mia's neck and pulled her in.

"I can't not kiss you anymore," Skylar said.

Then, she did. She pressed her lips to Mia's, and Mia opened her mouth to her, inviting her in. She'd kissed two women and more than a handful of men in her time, but she had never been kissed like this. Skylar's hand on the back of her neck moved them even closer together. Mia's hands went around her back and stilled on the small of it. She was pretty sure she moaned, but she was too distracted by the feel of Skylar's tongue requesting entrance. When they finally pulled apart, Mia wasn't certain if the kiss had lasted for a few minutes or a few hours.

"I should get back inside," Mia said. "It's been a very long couple of weeks."

"I bet, World Champ." Skylar slid her thumb along Mia's cheek. "Call me tomorrow?"

Mia smiled and said, "Absolutely."

CHAPTER 20

"AT the risk of being embarrassed by my mother, I am calling to see if you wanted to grab some dinner with us tonight."

"Yeah?" Skylar asked.

She was cleaning up her apartment after the toddler tornado and was just about to conquer the kitchen when Mia had called.

"We're going to this diner by the apartment; nothing fancy. My mom doesn't have a whole lot of energy, so it will probably be quick, but if you want to join us, that's where we'll be."

"Romantic," Skylar teased.

"I know. I'm sorry." Mia chuckled. "You can say no. This is not exactly the first date I'd planned."

"You'd planned a first date?" Skylar asked, stopping her cleaning.

"Not specifically. I just mean that I…"

"You thought about it," Skylar finished for her.

"A lot."

"Me too."

Mia cleared her throat and said, "We can do that part later if you want."

"You mean, after your mom leaves?"

"You know what you're getting into, right? I mean, I know we just kissed. We're not… It's just that I have a kid, and–"

"How about I just meet you at the diner tonight? We'll take it from there, Mia. Okay?"

"Okay," Mia replied.

"Now, tell me why you think your mother is going to embarrass you," Skylar teased.

***

"How does it feel?" the doctor asked.

"Good," Skylar replied.

"That's probably because of the steroid, which is why I didn't want to give you the injection. We won't know for a while if your pain comes back because of that." She squeezed Skylar's hand and wrist.

"It'll get me through the rest of the season. I'm holding up my end of the deal. I've been to PT every day."

"I know. I've seen the reports." She let go of Skylar's hand. "Stand up for me." Skylar did. "Now, get in your catcher's stance."

"What?"

"Just go with me here. I'm trying to see if I can clear you to play, Skylar."

Skylar moved into her crouched position. Then, the doctor used her foot to try to knock her over. Skylar pressed her hand to the floor to steady herself.

"Hey!"

"How does it feel now?" the doctor asked.

Skylar looked up at her and then down at the flat hand on the floor and the wrist holding it there.

"Fine."

"Honestly?"

"Honestly, it feels okay."

"Go through your throwing motion. That's where you had the most problems, right?"

"Yeah."

Skylar pretended to throw from a crouched position and then from a standing position a few times.

"Anything?"

"A little tightness."

"That could be from it being wrapped and braced all the time." She paused. "I'll sign the release. You can play, but you're continuing every other day PT until the end of the season, either here or on the road when you're traveling.

147

After the season is over, we'll talk about plans for the off-season."

"Thank you." Skylar let out a deep sigh of relief.

***

Skylar was feeling pretty good today. She'd woken up with the memory of kissing Mia for the first time, and just the thought of it had been enough for her to get turned on again. Then, she'd gone to the doctor and received great news. She had called Cheryl immediately after and told her she would be ready for the next practice. Then, she stopped by Megan's office with a fresh batch of scouting reports to debrief and sat down in the chair in front of her to go over them.

"Two from UCLA, one from USC, and two from Florida State," Megan said.

"So far."

"One catcher," Megan replied, glancing up at her.

"She's only a junior, but her instincts are good. I watched ten games she played in, and no one stole on her. Her throws to second were right on target every time."

"I just meant that I'm surprised you're bringing me a catcher."

"Why?"

"Because that's your position."

"I'm a scout, Megan. I can't be biased."

"True, but lesser people would have tried."

"Maybe, but it's not about me. It's about the team. You know I really only care about that in the end, right? It's my dream to be a part of it, but I–"

"I know that, Sky. It's one of the reasons I want you there with us, and not just as a coach."

"I'm sorry I let you down at the tournament."

"You don't have to apologize. You just have to tell me if your wrist is recovering or not. If not, I don't think there's anything I can do. If so, we can play things by ear. You might be a better catcher than you were a pitcher, and you were a good pitcher, Sky."

"It's feeling better. I've been resting it. The season is almost over. I'll know more about whether or not it's going to get better then."

"We have a few friendly games coming up. Canada is coming here. Then, we're going to Mexico. After that, Spain is coming here. It's my chance to try out some of these players you're scouting and see if any of them can play at this level. The games are during your off-season. If I put you on the roster, can you play?"

"Yes," Skylar stated definitively.

"They're friendlies, so I can bring twenty-five players. I've already selected fifteen. You pick the other ten. Send me the report with your rationale by the end of this week. That'll help me put together the final rosters."

"Okay," she replied.

***

"Sky!" Hazel shouted when Skylar approached their booth.

"Haze!" Sky mock-shouted back to the toddler in the high chair.

"Hey," Mia said, standing up to greet her. "We just got here a minute ago."

"Hello, Skylar," Mia's mom said without standing.

"Thank you for inviting me." Skylar looked down and gave the woman a smile.

"Do you want to slide inside so I can sit on the end with her?" Mia asked, pointing at Hazel.

"Sky, sit by me," Hazel said.

Skylar checked with Mia with a glance.

"Sure." Mia slid back into the booth.

Skylar moved in next to her and looked at Hazel.

"What are you doing?" she asked the girl.

"Coloring." Hazel gripped a red crayon in her whole

hand and scribbled across the children's menu.

"I like coloring. Can I color with you?"

"Yeah," Hazel said and passed her the green crayon.

"Skylar, I heard you were a coach, too," Mia's mom said.

"I was for a while," she said, looking up at the woman to answer.

"Did Mia tell you her team won the state championship?"

"Mom, Skylar's team was *the* national team. They brought home a medal. I hardly—"

"She told me," Skylar interrupted her calmly. "First championship since you were there as a player, I read online."

"You read about it online?" Mia asked.

"I did after you told me. Seems like they weren't all that good without you," Skylar said, winking at her.

"Sky, color," Hazel said when Skylar stopped coloring to have a conversation with the grown-ups.

"Oh, I'm so sorry, Haze. Let me add some green here."

Skylar could see Mia's mom looking at Mia through the corner of her eye. The woman was giving her a knowing smirk. Had Mia told her mother about the kiss? Had she told her that they'd had obvious chemistry from the start? So much so that Skylar's own ex-girlfriend had noticed and commented on it?

"Are you ready to order?" the waitress asked, holding out her tiny notebook and a bright-pink pen.

"I haven't even looked yet. Sorry," Skylar said. Then, she looked down through the red and green scribbles and said, "I'll have what she's having." She pointed at Hazel.

"She's having macaroni and cheese that she'll wear more than eat, and chicken nuggets. Are you sure?" Mia laughed.

"My two favorite foods."

Hazel lifted her hand into a tiny high-five pose and said, "Mac cheese."

"Mac cheese for me, too," Skylar replied.

Then, she looked over at Mia, whom she expected to see smiling, but instead, she saw a serious expression on her face. Skylar's smile left her own face, and she listened as Mia's mom ordered her food. Then, Mia ordered with that same expression.

***

"There you go," Skylar said as she loaded Hazel into her car seat because the child had insisted on it.

"Thank you," Hazel replied with her sleepy eyes.

Skylar stared down at her for a second and smiled. She looked like a tiny Mia. She was adorable, and Skylar, who hadn't spent much time with kids, had already grown to love this one. She'd had a lot of fun with Hazel. They'd shared a pizza. Well, Skylar had eaten most of it. Hazel had eaten half a slice, pulling everything off the crust and then eating only that. They'd watched a cartoon Skylar knew nothing about, and Hazel had explained it to her as if it was the most important thing in the world. When Skylar put her to bed, she couldn't fall asleep herself. She kept worrying that something would happen to Hazel, so she'd checked on her at least ten times. They'd played and colored together the following day. Of course, Skylar knew there was a lot more to parenting than occupying a toddler for a day, but she really did love this kid. Even tonight, at dinner, when she'd burst into tears because she dropped a chicken nugget on the floor, Skylar still loved this little kid.

"Thanks," Mia said. "I'll see you tomorrow at practice?"

Skylar looked over to see that Mia had already helped her mother into the car, closing the door after her. Skylar closed Hazel's door so that they could have a moment to talk alone.

"Are you okay?" she asked.

"Yeah. Why?"

"You were laughing at first. Then, you got serious. You hardly said anything in there."

"I'm still kind of jet-lagged and tired," Mia said.

"Is that all?" Skylar asked.

"Yeah." Mia looked down at Hazel, pulling Skylar's eyes to look down at her, too. Hazel was making a funny face at both of them. "I should get her home. She's so tired, she's in her slap-happy phase and needs a bath before I put her to sleep."

"Do you need any help at home?" Skylar asked. "You have your mom and Hazel both. I don't mind helping out if I can."

"I'm okay," Mia replied.

"I'm back tomorrow, by the way. I got the all-clear from the doctor today."

"That's great, Sky." Mia opened the driver's side door. "I have to get them home now."

"I'll see you tomorrow."

"Yeah," the woman said softly, climbed into the car, and started the ignition.

CHAPTER 21

"Do you need anything else before I go to sleep?" Mia asked her mother softly.

"Do you want to tell me what happened at the car earlier? Skylar went from happy to sad in an instant, and I'm guessing you had something to do with that.'

"What? How did you even see–"

"A mother always sees."

Mia sat on the edge of the bed next to her mother, who was lying down, and looked over at the sleeping baby in her toddler bed.

"I have a two-year-old, Mom. It's not like I can just date anyone."

"I wouldn't say date anyone, but Skylar knows all about Hazel and even took care of her for you. She doesn't seem to have a problem with it."

"It's one thing to babysit. It's a whole other thing to date a woman with a kid, Mom."

"She seems interested."

"She is." Mia shrugged.

"Yeah?"

"We kissed last night when I walked her out to her car."

"She kissed you, or you kissed her?"

"She started it, but we were both involved."

"What happened between last night and today then, Mia?"

"I don't know. Last night, I kept thinking about how I couldn't wait to go on a real date with her. Tonight, I watched Hazel fall in love with her, and then I looked at

Sky, who's only twenty-five and has dreams that are a lot bigger than being a step-parent to my kid."

"When was the wedding? I must have missed it," her mother teased.

"You know what I mean."

"Mia, you never really dated much. Here and there a little in college. Then, you met Gregg, and it's been him ever since. Skylar is interested in starting something. No one said anything about a ring or step-parenting. You also seem to be interested in starting something."

"I am," she admitted.

"Well, start it, then."

"It's not that simple."

"Nothing good ever is. Look, Hazel is young enough now that if something doesn't work out with someone you're dating, she won't know. She'll miss them for a bit, ask you where they are, and that'll hurt, but in a month, she'll be onto the next phase or the next new person in her life. If you're going to meet someone and explore it, now is the time to do it, if you ask me."

"It's not just about Hazel."

"Of course, it's not. It's about Hazel, and the team, and you." The older woman paused. "Are you scared?"

"Yes," Mia whispered.

"Why?"

"Because I really like her, Mom." She sighed. "And the last woman I really liked didn't work out how'd I'd hoped."

"You were married at the time and discovering yourself, Mia." Her mom took her hand over the blanket. "You're in a new place now. You're happier because you're playing again. Gregg is out of your life. And he's left you and Hazel alone. Then, there's Skylar, who you always talk about on the phone as if I wouldn't be able to tell when my own daughter liked someone."

"I did not." Mia chuckled softly.

"Oh, yes, you did."

Mia looked back over at Hazel and said, "I should let

you get some sleep." She stood up. "Are you sure you're ready to go home tomorrow? We can always move your flight."

"I'm sure." The woman smiled up at her. "I get to use a wheelchair at the airport. It'll be a breeze." She winked.

***

"First game back… Are you ready?" Mia asked Skylar.

"I wish it wasn't against the Stingers, but yeah, I'm ready."

"Because of Tori?" Mia asked, looking down at her glove.

"No, because they're right behind us in the standings right now. Plus, we beat them pretty badly the first time. They want revenge, I'm sure."

"You'll be great." Mia placed a hand on Skylar's arm.

"So will you." She looked around the field and then back to Mia. "Look, I know now isn't a good time, but you've been avoiding me – except when we're on the field, so I was hoping you could just tell me if this is a brush-off and I should leave you alone or not, because it's been a week since we kissed, and we haven't talked about it at all."

"I know. I'm sorry." Mia noticed Tori staring at them from her spot in front of the dugout.

"What happened? I thought we were going to talk and see–"

"Tori is on her way over," Mia interrupted.

"What? I don't care about that. Mia, we–"

"Hey," Tori said as she approached from behind Skylar. "Long season, huh?" she asked Mia.

"Tell me about it."

"Congrats on the national team call-up and the Worlds," she said.

"Thank you," Mia replied. Then, she looked at Skylar. "Do you two need to talk? I can leave you alone."

"No, I just came over here to say that," Tori answered

instead. "Sky, it's nice to see you again."

"You too, Tor."

"Hey, are you ready? We're warming up," another player from the Stingers approached and stood next to Tori.

"Be right there," she said, offering the woman who was a few inches taller than her a coy smile. "I'll see you guys later." Then, she walked off, joining her team.

"Let's go!" Cheryl said loud enough for everyone to hear.

Mia and Skylar exchanged a glance. Then, Mia turned and headed into the dugout. For the next two hours, Mia pitched, and Skylar caught. The team's hitting had been on fire. They were up four to nothing by the third inning, and by the seventh, they'd won nine to zero. The Stingers had only gotten one hit off Mia. Skylar had also played exceptionally well. She had two hits, including a double with an RBI, and had thrown out two players trying to steal second base, including Tori. It was a resounding victory, but Mia couldn't shake her melancholy. At the end of the game, she made her way to the parking lot to toss her stuff inside and pick Hazel up from the babysitter.

That was when she caught sight of Skylar talking with Tori. She knew she shouldn't be jealous. Skylar had told Mia that it was over between them. She *was* jealous, though. Just watching them together made her jealous. They were clearly familiar with one another. Skylar laughed at something Tori said. Tori laughed at something Skylar was describing. It left Mia wanting; wanting to walk over to them, wrap an arm around Skylar's middle, and claim her as her own. She wasn't Mia's, though. They'd kissed but made no promises. Hell, it was Mia's fault they hadn't even gone on a date yet. She dropped her bag in the car and went to pick up her daughter.

***

The following morning, they played the Stingers again.

Kai caught for the first four innings, with Jenny on the mound. Then, Skylar went in when Alex Samford came in for relief. Cheryl wanted to give Mia the game off and wanted to see how Skylar could hold up since they were in the home stretch and nearing the playoffs. The Stingers had a two-run lead going into the final inning. The Boomers were able to get one run back, but they lost three to two. Mia hated losing. She especially hated losing the day of the family picnic that Tom was hosting. She rushed to the babysitter's, picked up Hazel, went home to take a three-minute shower, because that was all having a kid allowed, and changed into jeans and a t-shirt with a faded logo she could hardly make out anymore. Then, she dressed Hazel in a cute little outfit, grabbed her bag, shoving what she would need for Hazel into it, and hit the road.

The party was in full swing when she arrived. In the backyard, Tom and the others had laid out blankets, and some kids were running around them, playing tag. Mia saw Jenny and Kai sitting on a blanket and joined them, holding on to Hazel until she sat down.

"Hazel, these are my friends. This is Jenny, and that's Kai." Mia pointed to them. "Can you say hello?"

"Sky."

"No, Kai, baby," Mia corrected.

"No, Sky." Hazel pointed to Sky, who was sitting in a chair with a bottle of water in her hand.

"Oh, yeah."

"Sky!" Hazel yelled.

"Baby, leave Sky alone."

"Hey," Sky said as she came over to join them. "Hi, Haze. Can I sit with you?"

"Yes," Hazel said.

The moment Sky sat down, Hazel moved into her lap. Mia watched as Skylar plopped her into place.

"We just got here," Mia said.

"I know," Skylar replied, brushing Hazel's hair out of her eyes.

Jenny and Kai talked for a bit before they got up and walked away to grab some food. That left just the three of them on a blanket as if they were one big, happy family.

"How'd it go with Tori last night?"

"Huh?"

"I just saw you two talking after the game yesterday."

"Oh," Skylar said as Hazel played with her hands like they were toys. "Wait. Do you think–"

"I was just asking," Mia interrupted.

"Mia, Tori only wanted to tell me that she and one of the players from her team are dating now."

"What?"

"Yeah. You know how the Stingers invited us to drinks at Calhoun's after the game?"

"Yes."

"She wanted me to know in case I was going. She didn't want me to see them holding hands or whatever, I guess, without me knowing."

"That was nice of her."

"It was. She's a nice person," Skylar replied.

"Did you go to Calhoun's?"

"No, Mia." Skylar looked down at Hazel. "I went home to sulk because the woman I *am* interested in has been dodging my calls. Tori asked about you, though. She wanted to know if we were together."

"She did?"

"She thought we were together the last time she was in town."

"Really?"

"Apparently, we have chemistry."

"What's tree?" Hazel asked.

"What's tree?" Skylar said in a high-pitched voice and started tickling Hazel.

"Sky?"

"Yeah?" Skylar looked up at her.

"Will you go out with me?"

CHAPTER 22

SKYLAR WAS on cloud nine. She'd spent the previous afternoon sitting with Hazel in her lap and with Mia at her side. She had, of course, said yes to Mia's question. They spent the next hour playing with Hazel and introducing her to some of the other kids at the party. Hazel played with a three-year-old boy and a four-year-old girl and shared toys. Mia and Skylar had gotten some food and returned to the blanket to talk more. When Hazel got tired, she ran back over to her mom and hugged her neck. Then, she'd turned to Skylar and asked Skylar to take her to bed.

"That's supposed to be my line, I think," Mia had said then.

Skylar had laughed. After that, she'd followed Mia home and helped her get Hazel inside and into her bed. Hazel had fallen asleep almost instantly, leaving them standing in Mia's bedroom, staring at one another. Mia had pulled on her arm to take her to the living room. There, she had asked Skylar if she wanted something to drink. Skylar had wanted to say yes so badly. She wanted to sit on the couch with Mia, talk more, and share another kiss, but she hadn't.

"I shouldn't. I want to, but I shouldn't. I think I'd like us to go on that date as soon as possible, though," she'd replied.

"Me too." Mia had smiled.

"I'll admit; I'm a little nervous."

"Why?" Mia had asked, leaning against the wall that led to her small kitchen.

"Not because of what you might be thinking. Although, I am nervous about that, too. I think anyone would be in my position. Hazel's special." She had smiled. "I don't want anything we could have to ever hurt her."

"Neither do I," Mia had said.

"But I was talking about the team," Skylar had explained. "I've never dated a teammate. I have a policy against it."

"Have, or had?" Mia had asked.

"Well, you're the first teammate I've kissed, so I'd say it's in the past tense now." Skylar had smiled at her. "We have a game tomorrow. Do you think you can get a sitter for later, too?"

"I can try," Mia had replied.

"Try," Skylar had said. Then, she'd walked over to her, pressed her hand to Mia's cheek, and kissed her lips gently. "I'll see you tomorrow, Number One."

Today, Skylar was playing well. They were up by three in the bottom of the sixth inning. Mia was back on the mound, pitching fastballs that no one could hit and off-speed balls that people couldn't even see. Skylar only had to go to the mound for a visit once. Mia threw three balls in a row. So, Skylar went for an encouraging chat.

"Hey, what are you seeing?" Mia asked her.

"A seriously hot pitcher with a rocket for an arm. Why? What do you see?"

"Sky?" Mia looked around to see if anyone had overheard. "You can't talk like that during a game."

"You looked tense before. Now, you don't. Come on, Number One. Just get it done. I have a date tonight, and I don't want to be late." She winked at her.

Skylar walked back to her position, crouched down, gave Mia the signal, and then felt her hand burn when the ball hit right on target. Then, Mia winked at *her*. An inning later, they'd won. That put them two games up on the Stingers and three games up on Stars and the Orlando Knights. The end of the season was upon them, which meant that they could explore what they could have in the off-season and see if it was what Skylar thought it could be: something real. Skylar's phone rang just as she dropped her keys on her coffee table.

"Hey, Megan."

"Glad I caught you, Sky."

"Have you made your decision on the ones you're calling up?" Skylar sat on the sofa, awaiting the bad news that she would not be one of them.

"I have. I'm taking a few of your recommendations and a couple from some of the other scouts."

"That's good."

"And I'm going to ask you to join us for the three friendly games as well."

"You are?" She sat forward.

"Yes, Sky. I've been told by several people that you played well this weekend. They're only friendly games. In the grand scheme of things, they don't mean much, but we do take them seriously."

"I know. I know."

"If you play well in these, we'll keep you on for other friendlies, and maybe by the next big tournament, you're back on the main roster."

"That's amazing. Thank you, Megan."

"Don't thank me. Just play well."

"I will. Don't worry." Skylar paused, wanting to ask about Mia, but not wanting to at the same time. "So, what pitchers are you taking? Who am I working with?" That was a better way to get to the point.

"Well, Fitch, Connors, and Landis are all getting calls like this one."

"Mia?"

"We think it's better if we keep her in rotation. She's playing at a high level right now. We want to keep her there."

"That's great."

"Connors and Fitch are solid, too, but they're working to make the main roster, so this will be their chance to show what they've got for the first time."

"Understood."

Skylar hung up the phone. Then, she moved to her

bedroom to pick out something to wear for her date. She showered after, dressed, and then moved into her guest bedroom. She had only put a bed in the room because she had planned on getting a roommate, but she had never followed through on that. And now, the room was just a bed, a table next to it, and some boxes on the floor. She took care of what she needed to do. Then, she checked herself one more time in the mirror before she headed out to pick up Mia. She knocked on Mia's door only a few minutes later.

"Hey," she greeted.

"Hi," Mia replied, smiling at her.

"Sky!" Hazel, who was on Mia's hip, yelled.

"She really likes your name," Mia said, laughing.

"I really like her name. Right, Haze?"

"Right."

Skylar tickled her tummy, earning a laugh.

"Do you need a few minutes?" Skylar asked her.

"No, we're ready. I have her bag right there."

Skylar bent down and picked up the Dora the Explorer backpack, shouldering it.

"Let's go."

"Let's go!" Hazel yelled happily.

Mia drove them in her car since it had the car seat. Skylar waited as Mia dropped Hazel off at the babysitter. Then, they drove on until they got to a restaurant neither of them had been to.

"This has got to be one of the weirdest dates you've ever been on, huh? Pick your date up; she has her kid with her that you need to drive to the babysitter; then, we finally get to the restaurant. Does it take the romance out of it for you?"

"No," Skylar replied.

She gave Mia a soft smile she hoped conveyed that she didn't care about any of that. The waiter approached and took their drink and appetizer orders. Neither of them liked to drink while in season, so they skipped the wine and opted for sparkling water instead. Mia looked a little nervous as she took her first sip. Hell, Skylar was nervous, too. Never before had the dating stakes been *this* high. It was only a first date, but they had to work together. If it didn't go well, things would be awkward for a while. If it did go well, they had a lot more to figure out.

"So, it's weird because we kind of know each other already. I don't really know where to start," Mia said after they had their appetizers.

"I think we've already started, so we just pick up where we left off," Skylar replied.

"I haven't been on a real date in a long time, Sky."

"How long?"

"College." Mia shrugged a shoulder.

"Gregg?"

"He was the last guy I dated, yeah. I went out a few times once we were separated, but those weren't really dates; and even if someone in the universe would consider them that, I sure didn't."

"It's my first date since Tori," Skylar said of herself.

"You guys were together for, like, two years. Try about ten, and then get back to me," Mia said, laughing a little.

"I like your laugh."

"I hate my laugh," Mia countered.

"Why? It's nice."

"I don't know. Doesn't everyone hate their own laugh?"

"Probably, yeah," Skylar said, chuckling herself. "But while I like the sound of your laugh, it's more that I love what it symbolizes."

"What's that?"

"That you're happy. And if I made you laugh, I got to be a part of that."

"That's sweet, Sky," Mia replied.

"It's the truth," Skylar said and took a drink of her water. "So, your mom seems okay with the whole woman thing."

"Nice segue," Mia said, laughing. "And yes, she's been amazing. She's always been very supportive of me, and this was no exception. I don't think she was ever Gregg's number one fan, but I was still worried about telling her about the being-attracted-to-women thing."

"How'd she take it initially?"

"She had a lot of questions." Mia took a bite. "She wanted to know if I'd always felt that way and just never told her. She wanted to know how I knew because, at that point, I'd never been with a woman."

"Ah, that old chestnut. How can one possibly know they're attracted to the same sex if they've never been with the same sex? It's like they forget they were attracted to the opposite sex without that, too."

"I think it's just a question that comes out because people are processing. I think once they really dissect that one, they realize how stupid it sounds."

"Probably true for some of them, at least."

"She was great about it, though. She was happy Gregg and I were over. That was definitely part of it."

"I'm glad you two are over, too," Skylar admitted.

Mia smiled at her and said, "I'd hope so."

"Can we talk about the team for a second?"

"Which one?"

"You heard?" Skylar asked.

"Megan told me when she called me. You got called up again." Mia's smile widened. "That's awesome, Sky."

"It is. I'm feeling better. The rest has helped. So has the PT. I won't know for sure for a while, but I think it's going to get better, and I'm really enjoying catching. I especially enjoy it when you're the one pitching."

"There's sexual innuendo in there somewhere." Mia pointed at her and offered a wicked grin.

"I guess so." Skylar smiled back at her. "Anyway, I was wondering how you felt about the team knowing about what we're doing. I know it's a first date, but I can't imagine stopping after only one with you, Mia."

"Neither can I," she replied.

"Do you want them to know or not know?"

"I think I'd like us to keep it quiet for now. We only have a few games left, and we're on track to win the whole thing. I don't want to throw anything off. For the national team, I definitely don't want to give Megan any reason for her to leave either or both of us off the roster."

"Agreed."

"Maybe in a few months or something, we can fill just her in and see what she thinks. If you're not okay with that, I'd be fine keeping them out of it for longer. We're both working so hard to get to the next games, but that's three years away. Assuming this works, I don't know that I'll want to keep it a secret for that long." Mia paused and added, "If I'm being honest."

Skylar's smile widened, and she asked, "So you don't have a problem being out?"

"No. Why?" Mia asked with an adorable scowl on her face.

"I don't know. I wanted to make sure. We're not exactly famous for playing softball or anything, but I wanted to know how you'd feel about me holding your hand when we're walking down the street."

"I'd like that," Mia replied.

"Good to know," Skylar said.

CHAPTER 23

"WHEN Hazel stayed with me, I cleaned up my guest bedroom, and it seemed to work out okay," Skylar said to Mia as they climbed into Mia's car.

"Okay," Mia said, wondering where she was going with this.

"I just know you paid the sitter for a few hours tonight, and I was thinking we could pick Hazel up, and – I don't know – maybe go to my place."

"Your place?"

"Sorry." Skylar shook her head from side to side. "I shouldn't have said that. I didn't know the protocol, and I thought maybe that–"

"You want Hazel and I to stay at your place tonight?"

Skylar turned in her seat and said, "I don't want to say goodnight to you, Mia. We don't have to do anything tonight. I just didn't want to leave you at your apartment and drive home alone. I thought that if we could pick up some of her stuff, and your stuff, too, we could go to my place, and she'd have a room."

"And we'd have a room?" Mia asked, lifting an intentional eyebrow at her.

"To sleep in." Skylar raised three fingers. "Scout's honor."

"Were you ever actually a scout?"

"For a year or two, yeah. But, seriously, if you don't want to, I understand. I'll keep it clean, and if you think it's something you'd be ready for one day, it'll be there."

"I don't want to say goodnight to you either," Mia replied.

Skylar smiled. Mia couldn't help herself. She leaned over and gave her a quick peck on the lips, wishing it could be more, but she only had the sitter for another thirty minutes.

"Are you up for trying it then?" Skylar asked.

"Let's see how it goes. Are you sure you want to wake up and deal with a two-year-old tomorrow morning?"

"Are you talking about you or Hazel?"

Mia glared at her.

"What? I've never seen you wake up in the morning. I don't know how you act," Skylar added through her laughter.

***

"Sky?" Hazel said softly.

"Yes?" Skylar asked her.

Mia watched as Skylar carried a very sleepy Hazel from her car seat into her own apartment.

"You put me to sleep?"

"If it's okay with your mom," Skylar replied, turning her head to Mia.

"Sure," Mia told her, placing her hand on the small of Skylar's back and rubbing little circles there to let her know it was really okay.

"Read me a story?"

"Hazel, what do you say?"

"Please? Read me a story," she replied.

"Can I?" Skylar asked Mia.

"If you want to." Mia laughed softly at how adorable Skylar was being right now.

She seemed just as excited as Hazel was at the prospect of reading a story.

"So, this is my place," Skylar told her.

Mia looked around as she placed the bags she had brought from her own apartment on the floor. The living room was a living and dining room combination and, as such, was pretty large. The walls were white, as with most apartments. There were a deep-brown sofa and a chair against the far wall, with a light-colored table in front of them. Next to Mia was a very large television with bookshelves on either side that were filled from top to bottom, but not overly so. Everything appeared to be organized.

"It's nice," Mia said. "Much nicer than my place."

"Your place is cool," Skylar replied. "I also had months to find this place. You had a couple of weeks."

"I'm hoping to move into something bigger as soon as I can," Mia told her.

"Me too."

"Really? Why?"

Skylar rubbed Hazel's back when the girl placed her head on her shoulder and closed her eyes.

"I told you that I want the whole thing one day, Mia: the wife, the kids; all of it." She met Mia's eyes. "I'm going to need a bigger place." She made a show of looking around. "Probably at least three bedrooms."

"Why's that?" Mia asked, following Skylar as she walked down a hallway.

"Two kids."

"Two?"

"Or, one kid, and a guest bedroom."

"I see." Mia smiled. "Who's the guest?"

"Depends on who the wife is," Skylar replied, walking into the guest bedroom.

"Why?"

"Because if it's you, we'll need a room for your mom to stay in," Skylar said. "Also, you should know that I'm pretty upfront about things when I'm in a relationship. Toward the end with Tori, I wasn't, and that was my mistake. But, Mia, when I want something, I generally say it. It has a tendency to scare off some women, but I'd rather know in the beginning if what I want is what you want."

She placed Hazel in the middle of the bed; pillows

lined around it. She had set all this up for Mia's little girl. Hazel was already asleep, so there would be no story tonight.

"And what do you want?" Mia asked.

"Tonight, I'd like to hold you. Tomorrow, I'd like to wake up next to you and make breakfast together; hang out with my favorite kid." She glanced toward Hazel. "And see where this goes. Long-term? All of it, Mia."

Skylar went to the bathroom, which allowed Mia to roll Hazel over a couple of times to put her in her pajamas. Then, Mia grabbed her own bag and went into the bedroom, where she saw Skylar sitting on the side of the bed.

"I just need a minute," Mia said.

"Do you maybe want to watch a movie? It's not all that late yet?"

"Sure. You pick," Mia replied.

She disappeared into the bathroom, closing the door behind her and letting out a deep breath. One-night stands were one thing, but this was her first official date with a woman, and she was now in her bathroom, getting ready for bed. Skylar had changed into a tank top and shorts. Mia hadn't had much time to gather clothes into a bag. She'd brought a baggy t-shirt and a pair of sweats. What had she been thinking? She should have reached for that one piece of lingerie she had bought once Gregg was out of her life for good. She had tried it on in the store, feeling sexy for the first time in a long time, paid way too much money for it, and then had never worn the thing. It had been in a box she hadn't unpacked yet that she'd stuffed in the closet. She changed reluctantly, brushed her teeth and hair, and slowly opened to door to find Skylar lying on top of the blanket, looking at the TV.

"Hi," she said. Then, she looked Mia up and down. "You look cute."

"I do not," Mia countered and walked quickly around to the other side of the bed. "I'm wearing the oldest shirt in the world and a pair of equally old sweats."

"I like you in sweats. When we were in the hotel together, I found it hard not to jump you every time you changed into your pajamas," Skylar said.

Mia stayed on top of the blanket when she moved to lie down next to her.

"You did not." She chuckled.

"Yes, I did. You wore that pair of... What were they? Cheer shorts? Were you a cheerleader in high school, too?"

"No, I bought them on sale a few years ago." Mia looked over at her.

"They look good on you. They leave little to the imagination," Skylar said, looking over at Mia. "I do like those sweats on you, but if I had my pick, I'd choose short shorts any day."

"You wouldn't just want me to sleep naked?"

"Is that an option?" Skylar's eyes went wide.

Mia laughed and asked, "What movie did you pick?"

"I haven't yet," Skylar said.

"I'm in the mood for some good old-fashioned romance."

"I wonder why," Skylar replied.

"Can I maybe snuggle into you while you pick out one for us to watch?"

"Is the naked thing still on the table or..."

Mia moved into Skylar's side, wrapping an arm around her middle and whispering into her ear, "If you play your cards right, we'll see."

"Tease," Skylar replied, wrapping her own arm around Mia's shoulders and pulling her in closer. "Seriously, though, this is nice."

"It is."

"Mia, I know we're risking a lot here, but I think it's worth it. When I first saw your picture before the league even started, there was something there for me."

"No, there wasn't." Mia laughed off the comment.

"Yes, there was, babe; I swear. I've never felt that before; that sense that I was supposed to know someone I was just looking at a picture of."

Mia looked up at her and asked, "Then, why were you kind of an ass to me?"

"Two reasons, I think. One was that I wasn't sure you were as dedicated as I thought we all should be. I'd just ended things with Tori, who only joined the league because she thought it would be fun to do for a year or two until something better came along; and the thought that anyone on my team wouldn't be all-in just wasn't okay with me."

"I was all-in. I am all-in," Mia replied.

"I know that now. I judged you prematurely, and I shouldn't have."

"What's the other reason?"

"Oh, I'm immature and sometimes act like a twelve-year-old boy who has a crush on the pretty girl in his class."

"What?" Mia laughed against Skylar's neck.

"I picked on you."

"Because you liked me?"

"No, because I *like* you. Present tense, Mia."

"I like you, too." Mia kissed her neck. "You smell good."

"I get that a lot."

"You do, do you?" Mia ran her hand up under Skylar's tank top and rested it on her stomach.

"No," Skylar admitted. "Can you do that again?"

"Which part?"

"The kiss part."

Mia kissed the same spot while she stroked Skylar's soft skin with her fingertips.

"Better?" Mia asked.

"Yes," Skylar breathed out. "Again?"

Mia slid her hand up a little higher. Her heart pounded with every inch of skin she touched. Skylar's muscles moved beneath her touch, tensing and releasing. Mia kissed the spot again, earning a very small, almost imperceptible gasp from Skylar.

"Sky, should I stop?"

"Only if you want to," Skylar replied.

"Mama!" Hazel yelled from the guest room.

"Shit," Mia said. "She never wakes up after she's down for the night. What the—" She sat up.

"Hey, it's okay." Skylar stroked her back. "She probably just wants that story I promised. She must have heard that I have amazing reading skills."

"Oh, yeah?" Mia laughed again and wondered if she'd ever laughed this much with another person in her life.

"I give a good read," Skylar said, sliding out of bed. "Pick a movie. If she needs you, I'll grab you, okay?"

"Sky, you don't have to prove anything to me by taking care of my kid. I don't want you to think I expect you—"

"I already love that little girl, Mia. You should know that by now. She's adorable and funny and smart, and I want to go read her a story. It's true, I also didn't want you to stop doing what you were doing, but there will be time for that later."

"Mama!" Hazel yelled again.

"Give me ten minutes. If I don't come back, send a search party," Skylar teased.

Mia gave her those ten minutes. When they were up, she went to the guest bedroom to see Skylar lying next to her little girl. Both of them were asleep. At first, Mia thought about leaving Skylar there until morning but then decided that their first night together wouldn't end like this. She did stare at the two of them for a minute. Hazel was lying on her side, facing Skylar, and Skylar's hand was on Hazel's back. She'd likely been trying to comfort her to sleep. The book was on the table next to the bed. Mia didn't know if she'd read any of it to her daughter or not.

"Sky?" Mia whispered.

"Huh?" Skylar replied groggily.

"Let's go to bed, okay?"

"I am in bed."

Mia smiled down at her, rubbed her back under her shirt, and said, "Your own bed."

"I guess I didn't realize how tired I was."

"Watching a baby sleep puts me to sleep, too," Mia said. "Come on. Let's go to bed, Sky."

Skylar stood up slowly, looked down at Hazel, and then over to Mia.

"Do you think she's really okay in here?"

"She's fine." Mia took Skylar's hand.

"Last time she was here, I checked on her about a million times."

Mia melted at that.

"I brought the baby monitors. Would that make you feel better?"

"Yes," Skylar said seriously.

"I'll grab them from her bag. Go to bed. I'll be there in a second, okay?" She kissed the woman's cheek.

When Mia returned to the bedroom, the TV was off. Skylar was under the blanket and was holding the other side open for Mia to slide into. Mia did and felt Skylar's arms wrap around her instantly.

"I really like this, Mia," she said into Mia's ear.

"So do I."

"Don't get so scared that you ghost me again, okay?" Skylar requested. "Just talk to me."

"I promise."

Skylar kissed Mia's cheek. Then, they fell asleep.

CHAPTER 24

"HEY," Skylar said as Mia walked into Skylar's apartment carrying Hazel on her hip. "Haze!"

"Sky!"

"Are you two just always going to be doing that?" Mia asked. "Do I need to prepare myself?'

"I don't know. Maybe." Skylar stood, kissed Mia on the cheek, and took Hazel from her. "Are we going to the park today, Haze?"

"No," Hazel said. "The zoo."

"She changed her mind six times on the drive over. One minute, she wanted to go to the park. Then, she wanted the zoo. She said aquarium at one point but has now landed on zoo again. Is that okay? I have the stroller in the car."

"It doesn't matter to me where we go. I just want to be with you."

"Hazel or me?" Mia teased.

"Both," Skylar replied.

They arrived at the zoo about an hour later. Skylar helped Mia with the stroller, despite having no clue how the thing worked. She put Hazel inside, and Mia lowered the shade to keep her out of the sun. Then, they walked toward the entrance.

"Can I talk to you about something?" Mia asked after they'd bought their tickets.

"Sure."

"Gregg called me this morning."

"He did?" Skylar grabbed two zoo maps from the woman passing them out at the entrance. "What did he want?"

"He wondered how we were doing."

"Is that odd?"

"I don't know. It's the first time he's called since I moved. He's sent money but hasn't had any real contact."

"How did the conversation go?"

"Brief." Mia chuckled. "It kind of felt like he was checking in. He told me he got a new job, so he's making a little more money. He also broke up with his girlfriend that I was never a fan of. He said he's going to send a little more money next month."

"Do you think he has an endgame?" Skylar asked, swallowing hard.

"I don't think he can. The divorce is final. He terminated his parental rights, so he can't really try anything. I think he knows whether or not he ever sees her again is up to me, so he's trying to show that he's working on some things."

"That's good, though, right?"

"Mama, elephants!"

"Yes, baby. We will see the elephants," Mia told Hazel as she continued to push the stroller.

"Haze, do you want to see the elephants first?" Skylar asked her.

"Yeah."

"According to the map, they're over there." Skylar pointed to the right beyond the long line of souvenir shops.

"Team USA catcher, great reader, and now she's amazing with a map. I'm not worthy," Mia teased her.

"They have big pictures of the animals on here, so I kind of cheated," Skylar replied.

"And to answer your question, it would be good *if* I thought he'd stick around. If he asks to visit or to see her when I visit my mom, I'd hesitate. She's doing so well here. She's probably even forgotten about him already." Mia sighed. "On the other hand, he *is* her father."

"He didn't want to be."

"True," Mia replied. "And if he pops in once every other year, I think that does more harm than good."

"I hate that guy. You know that, right?" Skylar said.

"No hate!"

Mia chuckled and said, "I told her *hate* is a bad word."

"Oh, sorry," Skylar said. Then, she leaned down so she could see Hazel and added, "Sorry, Haze."

"It's a bad word."

"You're right," Skylar said, nodding at her. "Elephants."

"Elephants!" She yelled happily.

"Sorry."

"It's okay. She has a friend in daycare that likely picks up his language from his parents, so I'm being cautious. She came home one day saying that she hated everything. She hated the lamp, the carpet, the TV, the water, everything."

"What does she have against the lamp?" Skylar joked.

"Maybe she has better taste than her mom. I bought the thing from Target for twenty bucks," Mia said.

"What are you going to do about Gregg?" Skylar asked her as they arrived at the elephants, and Skylar helped Hazel out of the stroller so that she could get a closer look.

"Nothing for now. He didn't actually ask for anything. I guess I'll play it by ear, but I keep coming back to the fact that he didn't want her." Mia watched her daughter, who walked to the fence, gripped it in both of her chubby hands, and practically tried to squeeze her head through the bars. "I did. I do. I want more, maybe. I don't know." She shook her head. "I'd give up everything if it meant she was safe and happy. I want someone around her that understands that, and maybe I'm asking too much, but I want someone who would do the same things for her that I would."

"I don't think that's asking too much," Skylar said, meaning it.

"You don't?" Mia asked.

Skylar shook her head, took her hand, and they walked over to Hazel. Then, Mia picked up the little girl so that she could have a better look. Skylar stood behind both of them, wrapping her arms around Mia from behind and placing her head on the shoulder, not occupied by Hazel.

"I want that for her, too; for you." She kissed Mia's neck.

***

They had been dating for a week. Skylar knew that wasn't a long time, but God, it felt really good being with Mia. It didn't feel like a week. They had only shared a couple of heated make-out sessions, due to their play and practice schedules along with Hazel, but this was what Skylar had been missing. What was most surprising to her, though, was that it wasn't just Mia that she had been missing. Skylar loved being with Mia *and* Hazel. She had loved their day at the zoo and their movie night later that day. Hazel had fallen asleep in her lap. Skylar had put her to sleep in the guest room like she had been doing that for years, and it just worked. Not only did it work, but it felt right to her. She had moved some of the boxes from that room into one of the storage closets, and she had also bought a few toys and put them in their places so that Hazel would have a place to play when she was visiting or if Mia was staying over.

On top of that, both Mia and Skylar were playing well. They'd played the final three regular-season games, winning all three. Skylar had caught all twenty-one innings. Mia had pitched for sixteen of them, resting her arm in one game to let Jenny take them home. Skylar just played better when Mia was on the mound. She played well when Jenny pitched, but there was chemistry between her and Mia that obviously extended far beyond the field.

"Hey, Catch?"

Skylar laughed at Mia, who was leaning against her car after practice.

"Yes, Number One?" She hurried over to her.

"Are you free for dinner tonight?"

"I am."

"Can I cook for you?"

"You pitch *and* you cook?" Skylar teased.

"I do."

177

"I'm in," Skylar said with a smile.

"Your place?"

"Sure. But I can come to your place if it's easier."

"I'm going to go grocery shopping and swing by your place with everything, okay?"

"Okay. I'll be there and ready to be your sous-chef, or I can wash dishes; up to you."

"How are you at chopping vegetables?"

"Pretty good, I think."

"Yeah? Any knife accidents I should know about before I assign you duties?" Mia lifted an eyebrow at her.

"Nope."

"Good. I have a vested interest in those fingers." She winked. "See you in about an hour."

"Fuck," Skylar said after Mia climbed into her car.

An hour later, Skylar opened her apartment door to find Mia there with a large, paper grocery bag.

"Hey, I got it." Skylar took it from her. "Did you buy the whole store?" She laughed when she felt the weight of it.

"I wasn't sure what you had in your fridge, so I got everything. I also got some instant mac and cheese to take home because we're out."

"I bought some," Skylar said.

"You bought some what?"

"Mac and cheese, for Hazel."

"Not for you?" Mia asked her.

"I saw the brand you get her when I was at your place. I thought I'd be prepared for the next time she comes over." She hesitated. "Is that not okay?"

"Of course, it's okay, Sky. It's very sweet how much you like my kid."

"Sweet enough to earn me a hello kiss?" Skylar asked.

"Definitely. But, put the bag down first."

Skylar put the bag on the kitchen counter. Mia stepped up behind her and brushed her hair away from her neck.

"Well, hello."

"I have a confession to make," Mia said as she kissed Skylar's neck.

"Okay."

"You have been very patient." She kissed that spot again. "And I have been going crazy." She moved her hand under the t-shirt Skylar had changed into after her shower. "I arranged for Hazel to spend the night elsewhere."

"Elsewhere?" Skylar asked, finding it difficult to say much else.

"She made a friend at daycare. That little girl's parents said they'd take her for the night."

"Really?"

"I don't have to pick her up until tomorrow."

"So, you're staying here tonight?"

"I'd like to," Mia said, kissing a little higher up, close to Skylar's ear.

"And dinner?"

"Can wait," Mia replied.

"That's a good idea. I—"

Skylar was turned around and promptly kissed. She kissed Mia back hard, pulling Mia into her body. God, she wanted this. She'd wanted this woman for months now. She hadn't wanted to pressure Mia for this, but she'd wanted it every time they'd shared a bed this past week.

"Bedroom?" Mia asked, pulling back a little.

"Yes," Skylar replied, pulling Mia's shirt over her head for her. "Better."

"Anything else?" Mia asked.

She was breathing hard, which meant her breasts were moving up and down. Skylar wanted to see them. She wanted to touch them. She reached around Mia's back, unhooked her bra, and let Mia take care of the rest. When Mia was finally bare from the waist up, Skylar turned them around and pressed Mia to the counter. She undid Mia's button and zipper on her jeans and yanked the denim down. Mia helped her by kicking them off. Then, Mia reached for Skylar's shirt, pulling it over her head. Skylar removed her own sports bra and pulled down the pants she'd thrown on earlier. She pressed back into Mia, letting her thigh fall between hers.

"Are you sure?" she asked into Mia's ear.

"Yes," Mia whispered back.

Skylar kissed her for a long moment before she lowered her lips to Mia's neck. When they lowered still to Mia's breast, she took the nipple into her mouth and let out a moan. She had fantasized about these breasts. She'd touched herself to the thought of sucking on them like this. Mia's breathing picked up when Skylar cupped the other breast and squeezed.

"Now that I've started, I don't plan on stopping," Skylar told her as she moved her mouth to the other breast.

"Touch me," Mia instructed, taking Skylar's hand and placing it over her white, cotton panties.

"Fuck. I can feel you, Mia."

"Yes, you can. So, feel me," she said with obvious desperation in her tone.

It wasn't exactly what Skylar had meant, but she didn't need to be told twice. The coarse hair that greeted her, along with the wetness she'd felt through the panties, were enough to make Skylar press her own center into Mia's thigh.

"God, this is what I've wanted forever."

Skylar dragged her fingers through the wetness, moving them down to Mia's entrance and back up to her clit. Mia pressed her back into the counter, reached for her own panties, and pulled them as far down as she could get them and then rolled her head back. Skylar watched at first. Then, she pressed her hand to the counter, kissed Mia's neck, and moved inside.

"Sky," Mia let out.

Skylar thrust her two fingers up and into her slowly at first. Her thumb moved to Mia's clit.

"So much for the bedroom."

"Oh, we'll go to the bedroom," Skylar replied, sucking on Mia's neck right after. "Just not right now."

Skylar thrust her hips into Mia, sucking harder on her pulse point.

"I can feel you, too," Mia said.

Determined hands moved to Skylar's underwear, trying to pull them down. Skylar moved back a bit, letting Mia pull them down.

"Just let me touch you, okay?" Skylar requested, curling her fingers inside.

She moved her center back against Mia's thigh and rubbed up and down, giving Mia what she wanted.

"That feels good."

"Which part?" Skylar asked, moving her lips to Mia's.

"All of it."

Skyler stroked Mia's clit, curling inside her. Mia moaned and said her name. Muscles clenched around Skylar's fingers, and Mia came hard against them. Skylar pushed in deeper, thrusting faster, until Mia finally tapped Skylar's arm, requesting a reprieve.

"Fuck, Sky. That was…" Mia stopped, likely to breathe.

Skylar rested her head on Mia's shoulder, trying to remember how to breathe herself. She pulled her hand out slowly, earning a disappointed moan from Mia. She smiled, kissed Mia's shoulder, and then moved her lips to Mia's. She kissed her softly, lowering her lips back to Mia's breasts, and then, moving lower still until she was on her knees.

"Sky, I need…"

"Me." Skylar spread Mia's legs. "You need me, babe. And I need you."

Skylar moved her mouth to Mia's center. She licked through her folds, hearing Mia sigh happily above her. Skylar moved two fingers back inside her, lifted Mia's leg, and sucked her clit into her mouth.

"Oh, God!"

Skylar loved the taste of her. She'd never tire of being with Mia this way. She knew that. She licked and sucked Mia until the woman began lifting her hips away from the counter behind her. Mia's hand first landed on Skylar's shoulders, as if she would need to push Skylar away because the sensations were too intense; but then, one moved to the back of Skylar's head and pushed Skylar into her. Skylar smirked and then continued sucking and flicking her tongue. She didn't start with her thrusts inside until Mia was about to come. Then, she moved hard and fast. Mia's hips rocked against her face, and she screamed out. Skylar stayed inside. She continued to lightly lick and kiss around Mia's inner thighs until she could hear that Mia's breathing had returned to normal.

"I don't want to get up," Skylar said, licking a particular sweet spot on Mia's left thigh. "I love the sights down here." She kissed the coarse hair between Mia's legs. "And the smells, and the tastes. I love the sounds, too." She kissed Mia again. "You are so sexy, Mia." She kissed her clit, and Mia jerked in response. "So sexy." Skylar licked her softly. Mia moaned. She licked her a little harder. "I love how wet you are for me."

"I can't help it," Mia finally said.

"Don't." Skylar kissed her clit again. "Let me have you again," Skylar requested.

"I can barely stand," Mia replied with a chuckle.

"Then, sit on the counter." Skylar suggested and kissed the inside of her thigh.

"We can just…"

"We're not *just* doing anything tonight, Mia." Skylar looked up at her. "We're doing everything. Let me make love to you for hours. It's all I want."

"And what about me?"

"You can have your way with me, too." Skylar stood, grabbed Mia's waist, and helped her onto the counter, shoving the grocery bag aside. She then lifted Mia's leg and kissed from the inside of her knee to the inside of her thigh. "But I need you again," she added.

Mia didn't argue. She spread her legs again, letting Skylar kiss her skin before she finally took her again with her mouth. Skylar leaned over her, using her chin to press into Mia. She felt Mia's wetness coating that chin and couldn't believe she'd gotten this lucky. Mia held on to her shoulders, trying to keep herself on the counter. Then, she came again, and once more before Skylar finally stood up to stare down at her. She wiped her mouth and slid her fingers back inside Mia, feeling how open and ready she still was.

"Sky, do it. Don't stop."

Skylar grabbed Mia's hip with her other hand and pulled her into her hand, alternating thrusts with curls until Mia came again. Then, she pulled out of her, kissed her deeply, and helped her off the counter with those still wobbly legs.

"Now, we can go to the bedroom," Skylar said.

CHAPTER 25

MIA couldn't get enough. Her body was jelly. It was actual jelly, and she couldn't stop touching Skylar. She lifted her head to look up at the woman, whose head was still back. Her eyes were closed. She had a thin sheen of sweat on her skin, which only made Mia want her more. So, she licked Skylar again, sliding two fingers inside her.

"Jesus! You just finished," Skylar said.

"Have you seen your body, Skylar Donahue? I just started touching it. I don't think I can stop."

This was so different than her previous experiences with the two women she'd been with. Not only were the orgasms out of this world, there were many, many of them, and they were all because of this woman. She'd been interested in Skylar from the beginning. They'd built this relationship at first from teammates to friends, and now, from friends to lovers. The orgasms Mia had given herself while dreaming of this night hadn't even come close. The sex she'd thought had been mind-blowing, wasn't even in the same universe with this sex. It had been hours of fast touches mixed with slow, sweet ones. They still hadn't made it to the kitchen for dinner. The meat Mia had bought for dinner would have to be thrown out, but that didn't matter.

"Mia," Skylar said as she came in Mia's mouth.

Mia let her ride it out before she kissed her inner thighs, moved to kneel in front of her, and tapped Skylar's legs in order to get them to move together. Then, she straddled her hips.

"I can't decide what I like more: me touching you or

you touching me." Mia ran her fingertips over Sky's flat stomach.

"Well, it's been several minutes now since I've touched you, so you might not remember how good it felt." Sky slid her hand between them and moved into her instantly. "Allow me to remind you."

"Oh, I'll never forget how good it feels."

"Because I'll never let you."

Skylar thrust inside her. She sat up and wrapped her other arm around Mia, holding her against her as she moved her fingers. Skylar's sweaty body against her own was hot in a whole other way. Mia let Skylar take her for what felt like the hundredth time that night. Her body was sore. She was exhausted, but she couldn't help herself. She wanted more of this. She wanted more of Skylar. When she came, it was with Skylar sucking on her nipple and pressing her thumb against Mia's clit. Mia rode out her orgasm. Then, she crashed into Skylar, who lay back down and held Mia against her body. Mia rolled off of her some minutes later. Skylar wrapped an arm around her and pulled her back in. Mia remembered what Skylar had said about this kind of sex, and she laughed against Skylar's chest.

"What?" Skylar asked.

"This is what you were talking about that day, wasn't it?" Mia placed her hand over Skylar's center.

"Maybe," Skylar replied.

"My entire body is sore. I don't think I can go again, but then I can't seem to stop my hand from moving here." She moved into Skylar's folds.

"Yeah, that's what I meant."

"So, it's been this way for you before?" Mia asked, applying slow, light touches to Skylar's likely still-sensitive clit.

"It has never been like *this* for me before, Mia."

"You know you don't have to say that, right?"

"If I thought I *had* to say it, I wouldn't have. I'm saying it because that's how I feel."

Mia moved her finger a little faster.

"How else do you feel?"

"Well, right now, I'm feeling pretty good all over."

"Yeah? Any particular place feel better than the others?" Mia teased as she stroked faster.

"My heart," Skylar said.

Mia stopped her finger. She lifted up to look down at the woman and smiled. She kissed Skylar's lips next.

"Mine too."

Then, she moved her finger again, bringing Skylar another release.

"It's two in the morning," Skylar said after she'd come down.

"I don't think I've been up at two in the morning since I had middle of the night feedings."

"What's that like?" Skylar asked, stroking Mia's back.

"Exhausting," Mia answered honestly.

"I hate that you had to do all of that alone, babe." She kissed the top of Mia's head.

"Well, I was the one with milk trying to shoot out my boobs, so even if Gregg was around, he couldn't exactly help with that." She kissed Skylar's breast.

"It sounds like he couldn't exactly help with anything," Skylar replied.

Mia looked down at her and said, "I'm ready to drop the topic of four AM feedings and my ex-husband if you are."

Skylar smiled up at her and asked, "Are you hungry?"

"Starving. But the food I brought has been sitting out all night."

"You know what doesn't go bad even in an apocalypse?"

"Mac and cheese, with powder claiming to be cheese?" Mia guessed.

"And it takes like two minutes to make." Skylar sat up. "I'll go make us some and bring water, too; lots and lots of water."

"After we eat, want to hop in the shower?"

Skylar stood up and stretched. Mia took in the wildly attractive view.

"Shower sex it is," Skylar said.

"That's not what–"

Skylar turned to walk out and yelled, "Shower sex it is!" Her arms went into the air as if she was celebrating a victory.

Mia cackled, she laughed so hard.

***

"I could go with you; take you two to lunch," Skylar said as she kissed Mia's neck.

"I promised her I'd take her to the park today," Mia replied. "And I'm regretting that because I got no sleep, and I feel like I can barely walk."

"I could go to the park."

"Don't you have work to do?"

"I have some scouting tapes to watch, yes." Skylar looked at Mia. "But, I can do those tonight."

"Sky, I'm taking her to the park for like an hour. She'll get tired and frustrated because she's too young to play with the big kids. Then, I'm going home because I have some work to do myself."

"Little league?"

"Yes, they're nice enough to let me work from home when I need to."

"What if we tried a little experiment?" Skylar suggested.

"Didn't we do that on your table around five in the morning?"

"I have film to watch. You have work to do. We could try to work from the same place."

"Really?"

"Am I being too clingy? I don't want you to think I'm being clingy. I'm just not ready to say goodbye to you yet."

"I don't think you're being clingy." Mia wrapped her arms around Skylar's neck. "Hazel will be there. She can be a normal toddler one minute, and then turn into a tiny monster who demands I get rid of the lamp she hates. Are you sure you want to subject yourself to that?"

"Fuck that lamp," Skylar teased, causing Mia to laugh. "And I know *fuck* is a bad word, so I won't say it around Hazel."

"You know you can't stay over, though, right? Hazel and I are in the same room, and–"

"I know. It's okay. I'll leave before I turn into a pumpkin."

"Then, let's go, Catch." Mia kissed her.

***

A few hours later, Mia and Skylar were sitting on Mia's sofa, both with their laptops in their laps. Skylar had headphones in and was watching a player who was batting. She took some notes on a pad next to her. Mia was looking over the plans for the end of the summer party Little League threw for the volunteers and staff.

"Where's Hazel?" she said when she looked up and realized her child had disappeared from her play area in the small living room.

"She said she was going to her room," Skylar replied, not looking away from her computer.

"Oh, she did, did she?" Mia asked, standing up.

"Is that something I should have stopped?" Skylar asked, removing the headphones from her ears.

"No, it just probably means she's up to no good," Mia replied. "I'll be right back."

Mia walked into her bedroom to find Hazel asleep in her bed. Mia looked at the alarm clock on the tiny bedside table and noticed that it was around her nap time. God, she had a really good kid. Then, she noticed a piece of paper at the end of the toddler bed. She picked it up and saw the stick figures Hazel had drawn with a couple of blobs as heads. Two of the larger stick figures were holding hands, or sticks, technically. The other figure was smaller.

"Mommy," Hazel said softly.

"Hey, baby." Mia sat on the edge of the bed, wiping the hair from her eyes. "Did you put yourself to bed?"

"That's my picture." She pointed.

"I know. I was just putting it on my bed so that you don't kick it off."

"It's for Sky."

"The picture is for Sky?"

"Yes."

Mia picked up the drawing, held it to Hazel, and asked, "Is this Sky?" She pointed to one of the large figures.

"That's you." Hazel pointed at the other figure. "That's Sky."

"Right. I can see it. It's very pretty. Do you want me to put it on the fridge?"

"It's for Sky," she said adamantly.

"Okay. I'll give it to her. Are you still tired?"

"Yes."

Hazel lifted her blanket to her neck and closed her eyes. Mia resisted the urge to laugh, leaned over to kiss her, and stood.

"Sleep well. I love you."

She walked back to the living room and found Sky looking up at her expectantly.

"She said this belongs to you." Mia passed her the picture.

"She made this for *me?*" Skylar asked.

"She did. That's me." Mia pointed. "And that's you." She pointed at the other large figure. "My guess is that the little one is her." Mia sat down next to her.

Skylar smiled and looked over at Mia.

"On a scale of one to ten... How freaked out are you that she's got us basically holding hands here?"

Mia kissed her and said, "I'm okay. I'm a little

surprised, but I'm okay." She then lifted Skylar's hand and kissed the back of the palm. "I think she's as crazy about you as I am; in a very different way, of course."

"Of course," Skylar said. "I'm crazy about both of you, too."

"She's taking a nap," Mia replied suggestively. "I closed the door when I left, and the baby monitor is on, so we'll hear her coming."

"Really?" Skylar said.

Mia moved into Skylar's lap and replied, "I don't know if we should get naked or anything, but I'm down to maybe let you get to second base."

"Third base or no deal, Number One," Skylar replied, unbuttoning Mia's jeans.

"I'll let you score a home run if you can do it quickly."

"You can't rush perfection, baby."

Skylar unzipped Mia's jeans. As she slid inside Mia's underwear, she winced.

"Hey, are you okay?"

"All good. Your zipper tried to attack me," she said, kissing Mia's neck.

CHAPTER 26

SKYLAR rubbed her wrist. She had been rubbing her wrist over and over for the past few weeks. When Mia looked her way and gave her a smile, she stopped. She smiled back at her, packed her gear, and headed to join the rest of the team. The Boomers had just won the inaugural championship game, beating the Knights who had come from behind the Stingers to make it to the final game of the year.

Unfortunately for Skylar, the last few games in combination with the nearly nightly sex with her amazing girlfriend had caused her wrist to start hurting again. She had already been to the doctor who had told her she'd only give her one more injection, but only after the season since Skylar had promised she'd rest it.

Skylar had then made it to the national team's test roster, which meant she had at least three upcoming games to make it through. Her wrist was aching in a major way. She could feel the tension in the tendons, and she knew she needed to rest it, but the two best-ever things to happen to her were happening at the same time. Both of those things involved her wrist. She and Mia had other ways of having sex, of course. Mia loved Skylar's mouth, and she seemed to like the few toys they'd tried, but Skylar loved driving her fingers inside Mia and making her come. That might just be the best thing in the world.

Well, that was different. Skylar couldn't think of anything she'd loved more than softball. That was probably terrible of her, but it was the truth. If Tori would have asked her to follow her somewhere after Skylar had gotten the Boomers role, Skylar would have said no. If Mia asked her to go anywhere, softball or no softball, Skylar was pretty certain she'd say yes.

NICOLE PYLAND

"You ready for tomorrow?" Mia asked.

"We just won *this* game, and you're thinking about tomorrow?" Skylar said back.

"It's your first game back on Team USA. It's important."

"I know, but it's only a friendly. It's just a chance for Megan to see what the college kids have. She's checking to see if my wrist really is better, more than anything."

"Hey, I promised Hazel a movie night tonight. Would you like to come over and watch it with us?" Mia asked her softly to avoid prying ears.

"I'd love to, but we can do it at my place if you want, and you can stay over. I actually have a surprise for you." Skylar smiled at her.

"You do?" Mia leaned in a little. "Does it involve us both being naked?"

"No, but we can definitely do that." Sky nodded.

Mia smiled and said, "Then, it's a date."

Skylar loved dates with Mia. Sometimes, they were with Hazel in tow, and other times, they were alone while the girl was with a babysitter. It was those times alone that always ended up with the two of them in bed, exploring each other as if they had never touched another human being before in their lives. Skylar massaged her own hand again, thinking about how she'd have her fingers buried inside Mia later. She had tried using her other hand a few times with Mia, but Mia's sounds had been different, leading Skylar to believe that the orgasms weren't as intense, and Skylar wanted Mia's orgasms to be very, very intense.

"Great season, everyone," Cheryl began. "I think we showed the world what high-performing softball is all about. It's nice to be the first champions, but it's nice to be repeat champions, too."

The team cheered as they gathered around their coach.

"I know some of you have commitments through the off-season. We'll be calling you one by one into the office to chat about those plans, the plans for next season, and

192

we'll get the team together again soon to start training. Those meetings are mandatory, so please keep that in mind when making vacation plans, looking for jobs, and whatnot. Take today to celebrate. Tomorrow, the national team is playing right here. A couple of you need to rest up for that game." She pointed at Mia and Skylar. "The rest of us, as well as the Knights, are invited to watch from the cheap seats. It's not mandatory, but it would be nice for us to show up and root for our teammates."

There were more cheers from the team. Then, Cheryl dismissed them. Skylar headed home to finish her preparations for Mia and Hazel's arrival. She showered and changed. Then, she wrapped her hand in the same fashion the therapists used. She started cooking food she knew she and Mia would enjoy, and readied the chicken nuggets that were in the shape of dinosaurs and the instant macaroni and cheese she knew Hazel would want.

"Sky!" Hazel yelled when she walked into the apartment, Mia holding her hand.

"Haze!" Skylar yelled back, picked her up, and hugged her. "Are you hungry?"

"Mac cheese," the girl said.

"Yes, mac *and* cheese," Skylar replied.

"She'll get it eventually," Mia said and leaned in to kiss Skylar's cheek before closing the door behind her. "Smells good; whatever it is."

"Just pasta. Nothing fancy."

"Thank you for cooking," Mia replied.

"Sky?" Hazel asked.

"Yes?" Skylar looked at Hazel.

"Can I play with my toys?"

"Sure," she said, placing the girl on the floor. "Come on. I have something for you."

"You did *not* buy her more toys?" Mia laughed. "She has way too many already. My mom just sent a couple new ones. I'm running out of room."

"I didn't buy her more toys. I did get her a coloring

book, but that's because she finished the other one." Skylar walked toward the guest room. "I hope this is okay." She nodded inside.

"Paw Patrol!" Hazel yelled and rushed to the toddler bed in the middle of the room, complete with the cartoon's comforter, sheets, and pillows.

"You got her a bed?" Mia asked as she stood next to Skylar just inside the room.

"The guest bed wasn't right for her. This one is, and I got those rail things that keep them from falling off when they sleep." Skylar pointed as Hazel climbed up onto it. "Did I overstep?"

Mia was shaking her head. Skylar didn't know what to think about that.

"I love you," Mia blurted out. "I've only told one other person that, in my entire life. He never would have done something like this, and she's his child. I love you, Sky." She turned to Skylar. "You're making my daughter feel like she has a real home with you. Do you have any idea what that means to me?"

"I guess I do now," Skylar replied, swallowing hard.

"Mama, it's Paw Patrol," Hazel said, pointing to the pillow.

"I know. Who's your favorite character in Paw Patrol? Can you tell Skylar?"

"Skye!" she yelled.

"Yeah?" Skylar said.

"Skye!" Hazel said, pointing at a little cartoon dog dressed in pink with what looked like wings on her back on the comforter.

"The pink one; her name is Skye." Mia kissed Skylar's cheek. "You know what else I love about you, though?" she asked a little softer as Hazel started singing her own version of the Paw Patrol theme song.

"What?"

"You understand the importance of the game to me because it's just as important to you. You make me better on the field, but off the field, too, Sky. I love how you make me feel. Being around you is intoxicating and freeing, but it's also the first sense of home I've had in such a long time. You're funny and sweet, and you don't seem to mind that I told you that I love you for the first time while my toddler is singing a cartoon theme song in the background."

Skylar tugged on Mia's hand to move them into the hallway. She then pressed the woman to the wall and kissed her softly.

"She sings it all the time. I think I know the words by now. Well, I know her words more than the real words. I think she thinks one of them is named Lubble, but it's cute." Skylar kissed her again. "And I love you, too. I love all of this, Mia." She kissed her neck after brushing Mia's hair aside. "I want her to want to come over. I want you to want to be here."

"I do; and trust me, she does, too," Mia said, kissing Skylar's nose. "She talks about you all the time."

"How can you be sure it's me and not the dog pilot?" Skylar teased, running her hand down between Mia's breasts over her shirt.

"Well, when she talks about the cartoon Skye, she mentions flying and the issues plaguing the tiny town of Adventure Bay. They have a very difficult situation there. I mean, they have to rely on dogs as their police department, construction crew, fire department, air support, coast guard, and–"

"Are you sure you're not talking about the Village People?" Skylar joked.

Mia placed a hand on Skylar's cheek and said, "When she talks about you, she mentions the trip to the zoo where you bought her ice cream, pushed her in her stroller, and held her up high to see the koalas." Mia kissed her. "She talks about how you watch shows with her and how you read to her. No cartoon dog can compete with that, Skylar Donahue."

"I love her," Skylar replied.

"I know. She loves you, too."

"I love you, Mia." Skylar placed her hand over Mia's heart.

"Skye!" Hazel yelled.

"Do you think she's talking about me, or the dog?" she asked Mia.

"Rocky! Chase!"

"The dog. Let's go to the kitchen. I'll help you finish dinner." Mia kissed her again, and Hazel sneezed in the other room. "Hold that thought. She's sneezed a few times since I picked her up. Let me see if she's warm."

"Can I help?"

"Can you get the bags I dropped by the door? If she's getting sick, I've got medicine. I also brought her stuffed bunny. She'll want to sleep with that tonight, now that she has her own bed."

Skylar picked up the bag as instructed – stupidly with her wrong hand, and quickly slung it over her other shoulder, silently cursing herself. She brought it to Mia, who was trying to wrangle a still-excited Hazel on the bed to check her temperature.

"I'll get some Kleenex from the bathroom," Skylar offered after placing the bag down next to the bed.

She went into her bathroom and took some ibuprofen for the pain, deciding she'd check in with the doctor after the game tomorrow to see what was going on with her hand. She then carried the Kleenex box back to the room and placed it on the table.

"She's a little warm, but that's not unusual," Mia said. Hazel sneezed again. Mia grabbed a tissue from the box and wiped her nose. "You okay, baby?"

"Yes." Hazel glared. "Can I play now?"

"For a few minutes. Then, we're going to eat dinner," Mia told her.

"Mac cheese," Hazel replied.

"Mac *and* cheese," Skylar corrected.

"Mac *and* cheese," Hazel said.

Skylar smiled at her and gave her a thumbs up.

"Dinosaur nuggets?" Sky asked.

"Dinosaur," Hazel replied.

"I'll go make them and check on *our* food. Yell if you need me," she said.

"Sky?" Mia asked, turning to Skylar.

"Yeah?"

She mouthed the words, "I love you."

"Me too," Skylar said with a soft smile.

CHAPTER 27

"I'M SORRY. This wasn't exactly how I thought the night would go," Mia told her.

"Why are you apologizing? It's fine," Skylar replied.

"Really? We'd planned a very different kind of night." Mia lifted an eyebrow at her. "*Very* different."

"Mommy, I'm thirsty," Hazel said from between them.

"Okay." Mia reached over for a sippy cup and handed it to the sleepy and a little under the weather toddler that was lying between them in Skylar's bed.

"Is she okay?" Skylar asked, running her hands through Hazel's hair.

"She'll be fine. She doesn't have a fever. She just doesn't feel well. I can put her in her own bed when she falls asleep."

"She can sleep with us," Skylar replied. "It's okay with me. I'd kind of like to keep an eye on her if I can, anyway."

"You're turning into a doting parent, Sky."

"Sky?" Hazel said softly.

"Yeah?" Skylar looked at the girl.

"Can I sleep here with you?"

Skylar looked at Mia, who nodded.

"Sure, baby." She pressed a gentle hand to her head, likely checking for a fever, despite the fact that Mia just told her she didn't have one.

"She's got you wrapped around her finger, babe."

"So do you," Skylar said.

"If I did, my kid would be in her own bed, and you and I wouldn't be watching cartoons right now," Mia replied.

Hazel moved to snuggle Skylar, which she'd taken to

doing a lot recently. Skylar wrapped an arm around her and let Hazel rest against her.

"She doesn't feel well," Skylar argued.

***

Hours later, Hazel was still rolling around restless between them. Mia got a few kicks to the back, a request for more water, and then a request for something to eat. Skylar must have gotten kicked, too, because Mia woke with a start when she heard Skylar yelp in pain.

"Hey, did she get you?" Mia asked, sitting right up.

Skylar held on to her wrist first but quickly moved her hand to her hip.

"Yeah, it's okay," she said.

Mia looked down at Hazel, who was sucking her thumb.

"She's out. Let me take her to her bed. I'll be right back."

"She's okay."

"Sky, we have a game tomorrow, and neither of us is getting any sleep with this tiny bed tyrant between us." She placed a hand on Hazel's forehead. "She doesn't have a fever. It's just one of those nights. I'll put her to bed, stay for a few to make sure she's really out, and I'll be right back. Then, we can get some real sleep." Mia stood. "Can you help me get her?"

"Yeah," Skylar replied and removed the parts of her that were touching Hazel from the toddler's body.

"I'll be right back. Go to sleep, babe."

Mia placed Hazel in the toddler bed, wrapping her up in the blanket she knew Hazel would kick off in a few minutes. She waited to make sure the girl was out for the night, finally, and went back to the bedroom, where she saw Skylar sitting up, holding her wrist.

"Is she okay?"

"Are you okay?" Mia asked, sitting on the side of the

bed, reaching for Skylar's hand. "Did she hurt you?"

"No, I've been hurt for a while. She accidentally rolled on top of it, but it's been pretty bad for a couple of weeks now."

"Sky," Mia exclaimed. "Why didn't you say anything?"

"I should have. I'm sorry. I thought it would get better once the season was over."

Mia massaged the hand and said, "You're playing tomorrow, Sky."

"I know."

"Are you going to tell Megan?"

"I'll be okay. She's starting one of the college players. I might only come in late if at all."

"Still."

"I wouldn't mess up the team's chance at winning." She shook her head. "If it's still this bad, I'll tell Megan."

"Can I get you anything? Ice? Heat?"

"I have an ice pack in the freezer."

"I'll grab it. Meds?" She stood.

"Ibuprofen in the cabinet."

"I'll be right back. Lie down for me, okay? You need to get some sleep."

"So do you. You're playing tomorrow, too."

"I'm used to being up at all hours. I'll be fine."

Mia grabbed the ice pack from the freezer, the medicine from the bathroom, and came back into the bedroom. She handed Skylar the glass of water that had been on her side of the bed, passed her the medicine, and watched her take it before placing the ice on her hand.

"Sorry," Skylar said.

"I just wish you would have told me. Did you think I would have said something to Megan or Cheryl?"

"What? No," Skylar said, lying back a little. "It's not about softball at all."

"What do you mean?" Mia rubbed Skylar's stomach under the blanket after sitting back where she was a minute ago.

"Babe, softball is not the only thing I've been using my wrist for these days." She lifted an eyebrow.

"Oh, shit." Mia covered her own mouth with her free hand. "*I'm* doing this to you?"

"You're not doing anything to me." Skylar chuckled. "It's when I do something to you, technically."

"Then, we won't do that anymore."

"Whoa! Let's not get crazy," Skylar replied.

"Sky, we can do other things. We *have* done other things."

"I know."

"And you need to rest it until it heals properly."

"I will."

"Okay. Good. We won't–"

"Mia, I'm not going to stop what we've been doing together."

"Sky…"

"Babe, I love it too much. Do you have any idea how good it feels to be inside you like that?"

"First of all, you love softball. You–"

"I love *you*." Skylar placed a hand on her cheek. "I'll play in the game tomorrow. We'll see how it goes, okay?"

"Skylar, this is your chance to make the main roster. I don't want to be the reason why you miss out on that."

"You won't be. You're the reason I'm even in consideration in the first place. Don't you see that, Mia? I am a better player when you're out there with me. It's what Megan noticed. Cheryl and Tom noticed it from the beginning. I'll tape my wrist up tomorrow. I'll get through the three games, and then tell Megan if she wants me, she has to wait until I'm fully healed."

"And we'll make alternate arrangements in the sex department."

"No, maybe we'll take it easier, but the best part of any of my days recently is when I spend them with you. The best part of that best part is when I get to touch you like that, and you make those sounds I love. I'd rather do that every day than play another game of softball." Skylar's expression changed then.

"What?" Mia asked.

"Nothing. I guess I never thought I'd say anything like that in my life."

"That you'd rather be inside me than play softball?"

"I never thought I'd love anything more than softball. I mean, I suppose I knew that I'd get married one day and have kids, but that would be after my playing years were done."

"And now?" Mia asked.

"And now, all I can think about is how warm and wet you are when I slide my fingers inside you." Skylar sat up a little. "And how amazing it feels when you're pressed against me, asking me to go faster and harder, and the perfection of feeling you clench around my fingers because you're coming."

"Fuck, Sky," Mia breathed out.

Mia slid her hand beneath Skylar's shorts and underwear.

"I didn't mean for you to—"

"Keep talking," Mia requested as she slid into Skylar's folds.

"When you're on top of me, and I'm buried inside you, I can't think of anything else."

Mia stroked her clit and whispered, "Go on."

"Your skin is so soft, Mia. I could kiss it, lick it, suck on it for days. I love your nipples and how they peak when I suck them inside my mouth." Skylar gasped when Mia slid inside her. She reached for Mia's shirt and lifted it just enough so that she could see her breasts. "Lean over me," she requested.

Mia moved deeper inside her and leaned down, hovering her breasts over Skylar's mouth.

"You're teasing me," Skylar said.

Mia moved a little faster before asking, "Am I really, though?"

"No," Skylar said.

Then, she lifted herself up to take Mia's nipple into her mouth. She sucked on it until she couldn't anymore because she was coming. Mia let her ride out her orgasm before she returned her fingers to Skylar's clit.

"There's something you liked the first time we did it. It doesn't involve my wrist," Skylar said.

"We should sleep now," Mia replied.

"Please."

Mia smiled at her. Then, she stood up and slid off her shorts and panties. Skylar watched her eagerly. Mia climbed back on top of her and slid up until she was over Skylar's face. Skylar wasted no time. Mia's hand moved back to Skylar's clit, rubbing her as intently as Skylar sucked and licked. They came together minutes later.

"I love you," Mia said as she slid off Skylar and rolled to face her.

"I love you, too," Skylar replied.

"Now, get some sleep, Sky." She kissed Skylar's cheek.

CHAPTER 28

It WAS the top of the seventh inning. Sky was behind the plate with one of the up-and-coming pitchers on the mound. Mia had pitched the first four innings. It wasn't her best showing, but USA was up against Canada three to one. Now, this twenty-two-year-old was trying to bring them home a victory. The only problem was that Canada had one of the best base stealers in the world at first base, and Sky's hand was killing her. She had already thrown the woman back to first twice. She wasn't sure how a throw to second would go, and she knew she couldn't hit in the seventh inning. She'd bat fourth, so there was a good chance she'd come up again.

"Sky, you've got this," Mia yelled from the dugout.

Skylar didn't look over, but she felt Mia's words of encouragement in her bones. *Mind over matter, right?* She could get them out of this inning. She called for the curveball. The pitch bounced in the dirt before hitting home plate. Sky stopped it, but the runner had taken off anyway. Sky stood as quickly as she could without removing her mask and rocketed the ball toward her second baseman. It wasn't perfect, but it worked. She had thrown her out. She sighed in relief. The crowd cheered. Mia cheered. Skylar could hear the woman yell above all the others, and she loved her even more for it. She crouched again, called for the fastball, and received the pitch for strike one. Then, the pitcher threw four balls in a row. Skylar couldn't do this again. Her hand ached so much, it was hard to think of anything else.

With the runner on first base, the pitcher threw a curveball that the Canadian batter hit into shallow right field. The runner on first rounded second and slid into third while the batter stayed at first base. Great. Now, the winning run was at the plate. Sky walked out to the mound.

"You okay?" she asked her pitcher.

"Yeah, that one just got away from me," she replied.

"Number nine is up. She's struck out twice. Just hit the target. Let's get this out. I don't know about you, but I'd like to call it a game."

"Me too." She smiled.

"Good. You got this."

Skylar ran back to her spot and crouched again. She looked over at the dugout to see Mia gripping the chain-link fence. Then, she heard it.

"Sky!"

It was Hazel's tiny voice. She was sitting in the front row of the bleachers, being looked after by the babysitter that Mia had given tickets to as a thank you for taking such great care of her daughter. Sky was tempted to yell back, "Haze!" but she decided against it. She lowered her mask, gave the sign, and waited for the pitch that she knew would be in the dirt. When it landed there, she scooped it up, looked ahead, and saw the runner taking off from first to second. She faked the throw to second base, which was enough to make the runner at third take off toward home. When she realized Sky still had the ball, she ran back to third. Sky threw to her third baseman, and she tagged her out. The game was over.

***

"Haze!"

"Hi, Sky," Hazel replied.

Skylar picked her up and kissed her forehead.

"You are my good luck charm." She moved the girl to her other hip to keep her weight on her left arm.

Hazel just giggled.

"Are you ready to go?" Mia asked as she approached, carrying both her bat bag and Sky's.

"Carrying my things for me?" Skylar teased.

"Well, you're carrying mine." Mia nodded to Hazel.

"Hi, mommy." Hazel waved.

"Hi, baby. Did you see Sky play?" Mia kissed her little girl's cheek.

"Sky threw the ball." Hazel pointed and then looked back at Sky.

"Sky won the game," Mia told her. Then, she leaned into Sky and asked, "How are you?"

"It hurts a lot."

"Let's go home. I'll wrap it up for you, and we'll get ice on it."

"I'm going to see the trainer first, to get it massaged and x-rayed just in case."

"Okay. Sounds good to me."

"Hey, you two," Tori said as she walked over hand-in-hand with one of the other Stingers players.

"Tor? I didn't know you'd be here."

"Season's over." She looked over at the woman next to her. "This is my girlfriend, Maggie."

"Nice to meet you *not* in uniform," Skylar said, putting out her hand for the woman to shake and regretting it instantly as pain shot through it.

"You too. You killed it out there today. You too, Mia."

"Thanks," Mia said. "And this is my daughter, Hazel."

"She's so cute," Tori said. "How old is she?"

"Almost two and a half," Mia replied.

Hazel tucked herself against Skylar out of shyness.

"She's adorable," Tori said, smiling over at Skylar. "Was I right?"

"About?" Skylar asked her.

Tori gave her a knowing expression and said, "Sky?"

"You thought we were together," Mia replied instead.

"I did, yeah." Tori looked at her girlfriend. "Aren't they a cute couple?"

"Tori, we're not–"

"Telling people yet," Mia interrupted. "Sky and I are on the same league team and now, the national team. We're keeping it quiet for now."

"We wouldn't say anything," Tori said. "You know that, Sky."

"I know," Skylar replied, rubbing Hazel's back with her hand. "Are you sleepy?" she asked Hazel.

"Yes," Hazel said.

"Have you had your end of the season meetings yet?" Tori asked them.

"Not yet. You?" Mia asked.

"Maggie's staying on the Stingers." She pointed at her girlfriend.

"Did you get traded?" Skylar asked.

"No. I'm done. I left the team. I'm moving to Boise, though. It's one of the reasons I came back. I have to get the rest of my stuff. Maggs and I are going to get a place together there."

"Really?"

"Yeah." Tori nodded. "It's what we both want. I'm going to go to grad school up there and pursue pharmacy, like I want."

"That's great, Tor."

"Mommy, can we go home?" Hazel asked.

"Yeah, baby. We're going," Mia said, reaching for Hazel.

"Can I play my Dora game?" she asked.

"That's at Sky's," Mia replied.

"Home, Mommy," Hazel said.

Sky knew what Hazel was saying, and so did Mia.

"Your place tonight?" Mia asked her.

"I'll be there in about an hour. You have a key."

"Come on, Hazel. Sky's going to do something and then meet us at home," Mia said.

Skylar's heart nearly burst.

***

"Megan, can I talk to you for a minute?" Skylar asked after she'd met with the trainer.

"Sure. What's up?" Megan was sitting behind her desk, likely working on the roster for their upcoming game in Mexico.

Skylar sat down, her heart racing inside her chest. This was quite possibly the most difficult thing she'd ever done, but she knew it was the right decision.

"I can't go to Mexico with the team," she said.

"What? Why not?"

"My wrist is bad, Megan. It was okay for a while, but I need some time off; probably a lot of time."

"Sky, you know that I can't keep giving you chances, right? I have to–"

"Think about the team, I know. That's what I'm trying to do, too." Skylar swallowed hard and looked down at the hands in her lap. "I've only ever wanted a few things in my life. Softball came first. I was little when I started playing. I fell in love with the game and never wanted to stop playing it."

"I've been there," Megan said.

"It came first. Sometimes, it was the only thing. When everyone else was worried about school or dating, I was practicing. I was working out, running drills, and at batting practice. Then, I fell in love with a beautiful woman."

"This is getting good," Megan teased.

"She has a kid, Megan. The things I've wanted in my life were softball, a wife, and then kids. I thought I'd finish playing, find a nice girl, and settle down, but the nice girl turned out to be a beautiful, strong woman, with a daughter that I'm crazy about. The little girl falls asleep in my lap and hugs me when she's shy because she trusts me. Her mom is amazing, and she loves me back. When I was playing today, I tried to be in the game as much as I could, but I just kept thinking about the two of them and what they mean to me."

"That's great, Sky. I'm happy you found someone."

"I found my family, Megan. I just don't know what's better than that." Skylar shook her head. "I love this game, but I love them more. If I keep playing, I'm going to hurt my arm worse than it already is. I want to be able to pick up that little girl and hold her, and if we decide to have more kids, I want to be there for all of it and do the same with them. It's new with us, Megan, but I'm all-in. And I can't risk hurting myself further for them, and I won't risk hurting this team, either."

"That takes a lot of guts, Sky."

"Maybe," Skylar said, shrugging a shoulder.

"What about the Boomers?"

"I haven't spoken with Cheryl yet, but I'm thinking about giving her the same speech."

"You don't want to see what happens with your wrist during the off-season?"

"We're still training during the off-season."

"You could go on IR."

"I don't want to take a slot the team could use while on the injured reserve list," Skylar said, looking up at her. "But, either way, I need to talk to my girlfriend first. I didn't exactly tell her I was coming to see you right now."

"She'll probably miss you when she's in Mexico, huh? Good thing Spain is coming here for the last friendly." Megan gave her a knowing look.

"How long have you known?" She lifted an eyebrow at Megan.

"I didn't for sure until today. I saw you holding Hazel. It was just a guess, though, until you told me your girlfriend has a little girl. I put two and two together."

"Are we in trouble?" Skylar asked.

"No. You think you two are the first two women to

date on this team? I'm pretty sure there's at least one more couple right now, and I knew about Ferson and Jacobson before we went to Tokyo, too."

"Shit. You knew?"

"They're still together, and they cause me no problems, so it's fine with me." Megan stacked some paper. "I'm sorry to see you go. And your coaching position is taken... All I can offer is the scouting gig. You've done great work so far."

"Thank you. I appreciate that." Skylar stood up. "I need to get home and talk to her."

"Tell Mia I said hi," Megan replied. "And that it's cute you guys thought I didn't know."

Skylar laughed and asked, "Does anyone else know?"

"I'm sure *everyone* else knows. You two aren't great at being near each other and *not* touching. You know that, right?" The woman smiled at Skylar.

"I think that's a good problem to have, don't you?" Sky turned to go but stopped herself and looked back at Megan. "Megan, can I keep my USA jersey? Something to at least remember this all by?"

"Of course, you can. It's *your* jersey."

"Thanks."

CHAPTER 29

"I HAVE to ask you something," Skylar said after they had put Hazel to bed for the night.

"Okay. Should I be worried?" Mia asked as they followed Skylar into her bedroom.

"I don't think so," Skylar said, pulling off her shirt and bra to change into a tank top for sleep.

"Can it wait?" Mia asked.

Skylar turned around to see Mia staring at her breasts.

"Like what you see?" Skylar teased.

"Always," Mia replied, moving closer to her. She then helped Skylar unbutton and unzip her jeans. "And I noticed there's this perfectly solid wall behind you."

"I would love to do this with you; you have no idea how much. But, can we talk first?"

Mia took a step back, suddenly concerned.

"Okay. Now, I'm worried."

Skylar pulled Mia back into her and said, "I was wondering if I could watch Hazel when you're in Mexico."

"You can't. You'll be—" Mia stopped. "You're not going to Mexico with me, are you?"

"No, I withdrew from the team," she said.

"Until your wrist is better?" Mia asked.

Skylar shook her head and pulled Mia in closer, lifting Mia's shirt over her head and unhooking her bra, putting them chest to chest.

"It's pretty bad right now, babe. It's going to take months to heal properly. I can't have Megan wasting a roster slot on me."

"Paris is three years away, though. You–"

"Do you know what I realized only very recently?" Skylar interrupted her.

"What?" Mia asked.

"I had these plans for my life. I was going to play softball until someone pried the glove out of my hand. Then, I'd find the woman I wanted to spend the rest of my life with, settle down with her, and we'd have a family." She ran a hand through Mia's hair, still wet from the shower. "For as long as I can remember, softball has been everything to me. When I had no parents because they were always too busy for me; when I had older brothers that didn't want to have a younger sister; when I had hardly any friends; and when I came out because I was forced out and then abandoned by the girl I really liked – I had softball." She looked into Mia's eyes. "We haven't known each other all that long. I know this might seem like a lot to put on you, but I love you. I love that little girl in there."

"I love you too, Sky," Mia replied, pressing their breasts together and hovering her lips over Skylar's. "You can tell me anything."

"I made a consecutive plan. One thing would end, and the next would begin. What I didn't count on was falling in love with someone while I still saw the game as everything." Skylar kissed her gently. "Now, I can only see you and Hazel. I'm going to miss this sport so much, but I don't *need* it how I needed it before I met you. If my wrist was okay, I'd probably keep playing until Paris if I made the team or until I was ready to retire from the league; but it doesn't mean what it once meant to me. Hell, maybe that's what Tori was talking about all along, and I just wasn't ready to understand."

"Quoting your ex-girlfriend while you're giving a really good speech kind of changes the mood a little, don't you think?" Mia asked.

"Don't be jealous. She tried probably for two years to get me to understand something that took *you* only minutes to get me to understand."

"Sky, I don't want to be the reason you give up something you love."

"You're not. Don't you see? I'm not giving up anything for or because of you. I'm giving it up for me. I don't want to risk letting any team I'm on down because something snaps inside my hand in the middle of a play, but it's more than that. When I picked Hazel up today, it hurt my wrist."

"Babe, you–"

Skylar kissed Mia quickly and said, "I wanted to pick her up. I want to be able to pick her up whenever I want to or whenever she wants me to. She's only going to be this little for so long, and I already missed so much, Mia. I don't want to miss anything else. I know she's not mine, but it feels like–"

"She's yours," Mia interrupted her softly. She then pressed her forehead to Skylar's and added, "You're more of a parent to her than the one that helped make her, Sky. The way you are with her – it's like you were always supposed to be in her life."

"So, it's not just me that feels that way?" Skylar asked.

"No, Sky." Mia kissed her lips. "It's you, me, and her from now on, okay?"

"A family?"

"*Your* family, Sky." Mia wrapped her arms around Skylar's neck and pulled her into a hug.

"I'm going to quit the Boomers, too, Mia. I'll tell Cheryl in our meeting."

"Are you sure, Sky? You don't have to give it up all at once. You can rehab–"

"It's okay. I don't want to be in pain anymore, Mia. It hurts so much all the time." Skylar winced just thinking about it. "If I thought it would be worth it in the end, I might have kept going, but I think I'm just going to injure it worse, and I don't want that. What if one day we decide to have—"

"Slow your roll there, gorgeous," Mia interrupted.

"I didn't mean tomorrow." Skylar blushed.

"I know," Mia replied. "And if you're sure about all of this, then I'll support you however I can."

"Speaking of that; I'll need to find a job. Scouting isn't going to pay the rent, and my coaching gig with the team is gone."

"You'll find something." Mia kissed her lips again. "We'll figure it out."

"Yeah?" Skylar asked.

"We'll be fine, Sky. I want you to be happy." She placed both hands on Skylar's cheeks. "You make me so happy. When I was married to Gregg, I thought that was it. In the beginning, it was fine. I was in love; or at least I thought I was. When it faded, I thought that I'd missed my chance at the real thing. Then I met Francesca and thought that was love, but I was more enamored than anything else, I think. You, my Skylar, are the one I love."

Mia kissed her then, long and slow, until Skylar pulled down Mia's pants and underwear and moved them to the bed. Skylar then removed the rest of her own clothing but didn't climb on top of her. Mia guessed she couldn't put weight on her wrist. So, she climbed on top of Skylar instead and spread Skylar's legs, running her hands along the soft skin of the woman's inner thighs.

"I want to…"

"I like you in this position," Mia interjected as Skylar faded out. "We're taking it easy for a while, Sky. We're making sure you heal right this time, because I plan on those fingers being inside me night after night for a very long time." She reached for Skylar's injured hand and kissed the inside of the wrist. "In the meantime, you can make me come any other way you choose."

"Fuck," Skylar whispered out.

Mia then slid down Skylar's body, spreading her further. She kissed the inside of her thighs, sliding two fingers inside her just before she licked her clit.

"Sky." Hazel's voice came from the baby monitor on the bedside table.

"Shit," Skylar said.

"That's a bad word, Sky." Mia nibbled on the inside of her thigh.

"We should stop. I—"

Mia sucked her into her mouth and curled her fingers, earning a gasp.

"She's fine. She'll go back to sleep in a minute."

"Babe, she called for me. I don't want her—"

Mia sucked again and thrust into Skylar.

"Tell me to stop, then," Mia said.

"What? I—"

"Tell me you want me to stop, and I'll stop. You can go check on her and find that she's back asleep already."

"Don't stop," Skylar said, pressing Mia's face into her.

"Good answer."

"Sky," Hazel said again.

"Okay. I should go now. She's calling for me, Mia. I—"

Mia stopped, pulled out her fingers, and knelt in front of her.

"Go." She chuckled. "Just remember what I said about that one." Mia hooked her thumb in the direction of the door. "You are wrapped around her little finger."

"Hey, I'm still new to all this." Skylar sat up, found her shirt and shorts, slid them on, and stood. "I told you I didn't want to miss any of it."

"Including orgasms?" Mia teased.

"Oh, no. I'll be back for those. We don't have practice or games to play tomorrow. I'm keeping you up late."

"Oh, yeah?" Mia asked as Skylar walked to the door.

"You told me I could make you come however I want. I plan on trying at least ten different ways." She winked at Mia.

"I'm planning to get started without you," Mia teased.

Skylar hesitated for a moment, grunted, and then opened the door.

"Give me five minutes. If I'm not back by then, you can get started without me."

"Sky," Hazel's voice said again.

"Five minutes," Skylar said.

"I waited thirty years for you, Sky. I think I can wait another five minutes." Mia smiled at her girlfriend.

EPILOGUE

"AM I CRAZY?" Skylar asked into the phone. "Bringing a five-year-old and a one-year-old to a foreign country?"

"Where's Mom, Sky?" Mia laughed.

"She's in her adjoining room. Your children are about to drive me up the wall."

"They're not *my* children when they're acting out," Mia told her.

"Fine. I'll own their bad behavior. I did feed them both a lot of sugar once we landed."

"You what?"

"I'm kidding," Skylar said. "They ran around the room for about ten minutes before I put them in bed and gave them their tablets. Then, it took about five minutes before they passed out. Your mom was pretty jet-lagged, so I'm letting her sleep for a while."

"I wish I was there with you guys."

"No, you don't," Skylar said as she ran her hand through her son's sandy-brown hair. "He needs a haircut, by the way."

"He does not; he's a baby. And yes, I do wish I was there with you."

"Babe, you're about to play in your first game as an Olympian. You do *not* want to be here watching these two sleep while I try to figure out where we're going to eat dinner tonight."

"I'll text you the name of the place I found when I first got here. I did some scouting for you."

"You must love me." Skylar smiled and sat on her bed.

"More every day."

"Does it have mac cheese?" Skylar teased.

"God, I miss those days. She's getting too big."

"So is he," Skylar said, staring at their children with a smile still on her face.

"You know what he told me he wants for his next birthday when we were on the plane?"

"What?"

"The drink cart. He said car, but he pointed."

"What?" Mia asked again, this time while laughing.

"He, apparently, thought it was cool how they pushed it up and down the aisle."

"We've got a weird kid," Mia said. "I wouldn't have it any other way."

"Soon enough, he's going to be asking for a bicycle and then a car."

"Stop it. I don't want to think of all that yet. Just let him be a baby, Sky."

"Hey, you looked hot in the opening ceremony."

"I did not."

"Yes, you did. You make Ralph Lauren look good."

"If I was actually on the big screen, it was for like a second."

"Long enough for me," Skylar replied.

"I'm glad you're here, Sky. I miss you guys like crazy."

"We miss you, too. I made a little video I'll send you when we hang up."

"Is this a video I need to be alone to watch?"

"No, those are only for when you don't have a teammate as a roommate, and when there aren't two kids in the bed next to me and your mom a room away. It's just of the kids and me telling you we love you and that you're going to kick some ass."

"You know the Olympic village is basically just a

bunch of athletes having sex with each other between games, right?"

"You know you have a wife with your two kids who flew across the globe with her mother-in-law to watch you play, right?"

Mia laughed and said, "Yes, my love."

"Are you nervous?"

"Trying not to be," Mia said.

"Can I help?"

"You already are." Mia sighed. "I feel about a decade older than all the other players."

"Well, you're not."

"I know. It's just that this is it, you know?"

"It's a good way to go out, babe."

"Only if we win."

"Then, win. If you don't, you can always stick around and wait for LA in 2028."

"Yeah, right. I'll be thirty-eight by then."

"Still with a rocket for an arm, no doubt, Number One."

"How about I just go out with gold in Paris?"

"Sounds great to me."

"Sky?"

"Yeah, babe?"

"I love you. I wish you were playing with me."

"No, you don't." Sky smiled. "And I don't, either."

"Really?"

"If I was playing with you, that would probably mean I wouldn't have been able to take time off to have Ryder."

"I suppose that's true," Mia said.

"Mia, I made the right decision; not just for us, but for me, too."

"As long as you're happy, I'm happy, Sky."

"Well, I'm happy." Skylar looked over at her children and smiled as Ryder sucked on his thumb.

"I should get going. I have a team meeting in ten minutes," Mia said.

"Send me the name of that restaurant."

"I will. Send me that video."

"I will," Sky said, laughing lightly. "I love you, Mia Donahue."

"You love that that rhymes." Mia laughed. "And I love you, too. Tell Mom and the kids that I love them."

"Always."

"Bye."

"Bye, babe."

***

Mia watched the video of her wife and kids smiling, laughing, and waving while telling her they loved her and missed her for about the fiftieth time. They wished her luck, and then Skylar panned the camera around to herself.

"I love you like crazy. Kick some ass, babe."

"Ass is a bad word," Hazel said from just beyond the phone.

The video ended there. Mia laughed every time she watched it. She had two weeks of softball left in her, and then she'd retire. She didn't just want to win this medal for herself, her team, and her country. She wanted to win it for Sky, for her mom, and for her kids. Ryder wouldn't remember much, if anything, from this trip. Hazel would, though. She was probably just old enough to be able to remember the time her mom wore a uniform in red, white, and blue and represented her country in the Olympic games.

Less than a year after meeting Skylar Donahue, Mia had proposed. They didn't waste any time. Neither of them wanted a big wedding. Skylar's family didn't even want to know that she had a fiancée, so they opted to get married at the courthouse with Mia's mom and Hazel there. Not long after that, Mia did something that would make Skylar very, very happy. She got the paperwork drawn up and had Hazel present it to her. Mia hadn't ever seen Skylar cry before, but those were happy tears.

"She's mine?" Skylar had asked with those tears in her eyes as Hazel sat on her lap.

"She always was, babe," Mia had replied.

"But, she's really mine?" Skylar had checked.

"You have to sign the papers, but yes, she's your daughter legally and officially if you do."

"What about—"

"Gregg knows. He's fine with it, and he has no say anyway, Skylar. He gave up his chance to be her parent. You've asked for it every day for as long as we've known you." Mia had wiped the tears from Skylar's eyes, leaned down, and kissed her.

"Gross," Hazel had said.

"Haze, do you want Sky to be Mommy Sky?"

"Sky *is* Mommy Sky," Hazel had stated in a matter-of-fact tone. "Can I have mac and cheese for dinner?"

"Can I have some with you?" Skylar had asked her daughter before she'd kissed Hazel's temple.

"Okay." Hazel had hopped off her lap then, and for some reason, had run into her bedroom.

Mia had hopped into Skylar's lap instead, watching Skylar stare at the paper in front of her.

"It means changing her name to Donahue, too, you know?" Mia offered.

"Hazel Donahue?"

Mia had taken the paper from Skylar and placed it on the table nearby. She'd wrapped her arms around Skylar's neck and leaned down.

"Skylar, Mia, and Hazel Donahue; one big, happy family, babe."

"And maybe another one, too?"

"Whenever you're ready," Mia had told her.

"I'm ready," Skylar had said, wrapping her arms around Mia's waist and pulling her closer.

Ryder had come along not long after; they'd gotten lucky with in vitro. Skylar had been a beautiful pregnant woman. Ryder looked just like her, with a cute nose; and

God, Mia missed her family. She wouldn't be able to see them for the next few days, and even then, it would be sparingly. She needed to focus on the games. She could look at them in the stands, and that would have to be enough until this was all over, and she could hold her wife in her arms, pick up her daughter, hold her son, and hug her mother.

***

"Well, this isn't going how we'd hoped," Megan grunted. "Fuck!" she yelled in the office the managers had been given for the games.

"Everything okay?" Mia asked, stopping in the doorway. "Sorry, I just heard you yell. We *did* win today, Megan."

"Jayden is out for the rest of the games," Megan said. "That hamstring she pulled in our first practice is worse than we thought."

"Oh," Mia said.

"Elena is the only decent back-up we have in her position."

"And she's not been feeling great since we got here. I saw her throw up after the game."

"The doctor said it's the flu. She's tried to tough it out so far, but she's out for at least the next few games. Even the B-12 shots aren't helping. I can't have her getting the rest of the team sick."

There were eight teams competing in the games. In the first round of the competition, each of the teams plays all the other teams once. After that, the top four teams advance to a playoff round consisting of two semi-final games, and finally, the bronze and gold medal games. The USA had already beaten Australia and Venezuela. They still had Canada, China, Chinese Taipei, Japan, and the Netherlands left in the round-robin play. It was a tough tournament. The team would, hopefully, play ten games; the seven in the first round, then the semi-final, and the final medal game; either for a bronze or a gold medal.

"What are you going to do?" Mia asked, swallowing as she thought about Megan's option, silently wishing for the one she had never thought possible.

Megan looked up at her and said, "I've got Robinson at third base. I can move her."

"Sure," Mia replied with disappointment.

"But she's not a natural catcher. There's going to be an adjustment, and we don't have time for that. Canada and China won their first two games, too," she said, thinking out loud. Then, she met Mia's eyes. "We put her on the list for a reason, right?"

"We did," Mia said.

"She hasn't played professionally in three years, Mia."

"She's still catching for me in the backyard, Megan. She's still got it. It's nuts, and I don't expect you to do it… I need to take myself out of the conversation probably, because I'm biased, but she is listed."

"As an alternate, I know." Megan sighed. "I mainly did that as a gesture."

"She knows that. Neither of us expects anything."

"Let me talk to the coaching staff. Don't say anything to her, Mia. We have a lot of planning to do tonight before we make any moves."

"I won't. I understand. I wouldn't want to get her hopes up, anyway."

Mia walked out of the office and met the team where they were having lunch. The rest of the day, she could hardly think of anything else. Skylar hadn't returned to Team USA as a coach, but she had remained on as a scout. She'd gotten a college coaching job, though, and had helped that team get to the national semi-finals in her second year on the job. She was also Mia's catcher at home in their backyard. Sky still remembered what it was like to be a pitcher and helped coach Mia on her stance, her follow-through, and pitches.

Mia was dreading their phone call later, where she

would say goodnight to the kids and talk to Sky for a bit. She never dreaded their calls, but this one would be tough. Before they'd left for the games, Megan had had to name the team alternates. Skylar had been named more as a gesture than for any other reason, and she'd been incredibly grateful for that. It didn't mean more than her name just being on the list back then. The team had two amazing catchers, and Skylar hadn't played in years. Perhaps, Megan should have added another catcher to the alternate list, but she hadn't. Robinson played third for the team, but she had caught some in high school. Technically, Beauregard had been a catcher for a year in college, but she'd blown out a knee that season, and she'd stayed in the outfield ever since.

"Hello?" Mia said into the phone.

"Mia, I just got the strangest call," Skylar said.

Mia's heart raced, and she said, "From who?"

"Megan," Skylar said.

"Megan? Why'd she call you?"

"She told me you knew, babe. You don't have to pretend anymore," Skylar replied with a light laugh. "Babe, she called me up. She wants me to play. Because you're still in the round-robin round, and Jayden is out for good, I guess they can do that."

"We, babe."

"What?"

"*We* can do that." Mia smiled. "I assume you said yes; which means you're on the team, Sky."

"I did, but mostly because I hadn't thought it through. Mia, I haven't played in three years. I've had a baby since then."

"Hello, have we met? I'm your wife. I took a few years off, had a kid, and returned to the game."

"Mia, I'm—"

"Skylar, you can do this, babe. I'll be right there with you."

"What about the kids?"

"Mom can watch them."

"That's a lot to put on her."

"I'm sure she will do it happily if it means both of her daughters get to play in the Olympics. Skylar, you'd be crazy not to do this."

Skylar laughed and said, "I never thought…"

"No one did."

"There's one rule, though."

"What's that?" Mia asked, confused.

"Megan said we're not allowed to share a room," Skylar told her.

Mia laughed wildly at that.

"Get over to the village, Olympian."

***

Skylar hadn't traveled with the team. She hadn't brought any of her own gear. She was pretty sure it was in the garage somewhere. The team equipment manager handed her everything she'd need, though.

"Hey guys, most of you know Sky." Megan motioned to Skylar as the team sat in the locker room. "She's a member of this team in more ways than one for a long time now."

"Two Donahue's on one team," one of the players teased. "Bring it on!"

"Jayden's out for the tournament. It was a muscle tear, and we're going to miss her, but Skylar is ready to go. Right, Sky?"

"Yes, Coach," Skylar replied, hoping that was true.

"Take a seat. We've got a quick meeting before a light practice. Then, we're doing a team lunch, film, and the game tonight."

Skylar sat down in Jayden's old spot, which was a few spots away from her wife. She looked over at Mia, who looked back at her, nodding at Skylar's Team USA practice shirt and shorts.

Many hours later, after a practice where Skylar shook

the cobwebs off her arm, she felt good. Catching for her wife in the backyard had kept her knees and arm good. Working out with Mia most days and going to the batting cages every now and then had kept her in shape and form. When the game started, Skylar moved behind the plate, let out a deep breath, and took her position, crouching down. She then looked at the mound at her wife, who would be throwing some warm-up pitches before the game, and thought it felt like they were at home in their backyard, with Ryder in a baby chair and Hazel playing with her toys on their deck.

Elena started feeling better around their last game in the round-robin portion of the event. By then, Skylar was tired. She had caught every game, and the exhaustion of a tournament like this was starting to get to her. Team USA had won all of their games as expected. They had been the World Champions already three times in a row, including the previous year, leading up to these games. In their semi-final, they played Canada. Elena caught that one. Skylar got to sit next to her wife on the bench and watch the team win. Skylar figured she wouldn't catch in the final game, for obvious reasons. Elena was their full-time catcher with Jayden out. Skylar had been an alternate.

When Megan announced the starting line-up, Skylar wasn't on it. Mia was the starting pitcher, which was perfect. Skylar would get to watch her wife, hopefully, throw the last pitch in the Olympics and win a gold medal. They were playing Japan, number two in the world, and they were down by one in the fifth inning. Team USA's second baseman had made a costly error on a ground ball and cost them a run.

"Sky?" Megan called.

"Yeah?" Skylar said.

"Is she okay?" she asked, nodding to Mia, who did look a little tired.

"She's good," Skylar replied, chuckling. "She's in the zone right now."

"I need her to get us through at least this inning."

"She will. Really, she's fine, Megan. Trust me. I know my wife. Right now, she's planning the next ten pitches. Takigachi is up next. Mia knows to throw her low and away. After that, she's got Niu. She'll throw her high and inside."

Megan glanced over at her, and then her attention was drawn to the field, where Mia had just thrown a fastball low and away that Takigachi had let blow by her.

"See?" Skylar said.

"All right, smart-ass." Megan laughed and shoved at Skylar's shoulder.

In the top of the sixth, the USA tied the game. In the top of the seventh, they scored two more. Japan had one more chance to score at least two to tie, if not three, and they had the bottom of their line-up coming to bat. It was looking up for Team USA.

"Bring it home, baby," Skylar said, smacking Mia's ass.

"Sky, you're in," Megan yelled.

"What???" Skylar and Mia asked at the same time.

"Get out there before I change my mind," Megan said, pointing to the field.

"Hey," Mia began. "Three more outs. That's all we need."

"You don't have to coach me up, Number One. I just have to sit back there and catch. You're the one that has to hit the target."

Skylar put on her gear, grabbed her borrowed glove, and joined her wife on the field. She looked over to the bleachers and saw her mother-in-law holding a sleeping Ryder and standing next to Hazel. How Ryder could sleep at a time like this was beyond her, but it was Hazel's little wave that made Skylar almost melt. Yeah, she was bringing this one home with her wife for their kids.

"Three up. Three down," she said when she jogged to the mound before the inning started. "Ryder's napping against your mom, and I'm more than ready to hug my kids after we win."

"Then, let's do this already, Donahue."

Mia got the first batter to go down swinging. The second batter lined straight to their first baseman. That left Japan's number nine hitter, and Team USA was one out away from another gold medal. Skylar's heart was pounding. She tried to keep herself focused on Mia, and pictured them playing in their backyard again. Mia pitched a fastball high and outside. The batter let that one go. Skylar thought about her very first softball game as a little kid. Mia pitched a strike right down the middle. She thought about the times her brother reluctantly drove her to practice. Mia pitched another strike; swing and a miss for Japan. Skylar then pictured her time playing in college. Mia pitched low and outside. It was a ball that the batter didn't swing at. She pictured seeing Mia for the first time, watching her pitch and being mesmerized. She pictured Mia's face after their first kiss; after the first time Skylar had touched her; when Mia had proposed and heard Skylar say yes; when Mia had said, "I do" at their wedding; when Skylar had told her she was pregnant; and then just the other day, when Mia had smiled and hugged her because Skylar was wearing a Team USA uniform. She pictured every moment that led her to this one. She had no regrets. It felt like, to Skylar, that she had only miracles. Mia pitched strike three.